FOR GOODNESS SAKE

Anthony Wroth

To Simon, Jeremy and Hugo

Published by Raydon
42, Little Bushey Lane
Bushey Heath
Herts. WD2 3JX.

1994 Edition.

© Copyright Anthony Wroth.

ISBN. 0 9524206 0 0

Printed and bound in Great Britain by
Able Publishing Services,
9, Station Road
Knebworth
Herts.
SG3 6AP

CHAPTER ONE

Perhaps I should start by telling you who I am.

I don't mean all that stuff about one's antecedents - father a drunken bully, mother a long-suffering cello teacher, that sort of thing - because, in my case, it's all so very dull. Who cares whether one's grandfather was the seventh son of a seventh son, for goodness' sake?

No, I mean that if I am to present myself as the narrator of these chronicles, you have the right to know how I'm able to recount all the events and conversations that follow. I get very impatient with authors who don't explain how they are apparently able to take a god-like view of the sweep of a mighty battle at one moment and penetrate the most intimate unspoken thoughts of their dramatis personae the next. Take Tolstoy, for instance: he's pretty sound in most respects but he falls down badly on this score.

Unlike Tolstoy, I can tell you what happened next, and where and why, and who said what to whom, because I was there. Well, that's not always strictly true; but it's as good as being true because when I wasn't in the same room as these events, I was still able to experience them through my ubiquitous surveillance system.

Some people claim to be disgusted by such concepts as 'spying' or 'eavesdropping' but I can't understand their concern. Why shouldn't I be allowed to know what is being said and done in rooms other than those I happen to be in? (I exclude, of course, activities over which natural modesty would cast a veil). If the existence of walls is taken as excusing the utterance of statements which would cause offence to people not within them, should those statements be made at all? Isn't demand for 'privacy' an admission of a guilty conscience?

Well, that's my philosophical justification for my sight-and-sound surveillance system. A more practical raison d'etre lies in the fact that I am a professional business management consultant and that I have been the business adviser to four generations of chairmen and Boards of Directors of one particularly splendid company. (Goodness knows what they would have done without me!)

Now, an essential feature of business management is to possess all the intelligence needed to make well-based decisions; so it was my responsibility to acquire and supply such intelligence. And if I could garner my information by a tap here, a tap there, a concealed camera in an office, a pub, a church, a home... then why not?

I'm aware I cause a little mirth amongst the smart set because some of the technology I use in my information-gathering dates back many decades. But if it works, why not use it? Why employ some sophisticated, at-the-cutting-edge, up-to-the-minute, state-of-the-art hoopla when a pair of copper wires would do? That's not to say I reject modern developments - far from it; I have as much technical expertise as the next man when inventive brilliance is required. But, I have to admit, there are occasions when significant events occur beyond the range even of my widespread network.

A little earlier I dismissed as of little interest the fact that my grandfather was the seventh son of a seventh son; but I confess I'm not above exploiting this relationship when dealing with some of my clients. I don't know why, but a number of businessmen are uneasily conscious that they don't appreciate the arts and the other irrational aspects of life as fully as they might. In some crazy way of compensation, they are susceptible to a touch of mysticism creeping in amongst the balance sheets and quantified business plans: they consult astrologers, graphologists, that sort of thing. In my dealings with over four generations of businessmen there are many who preferred to believe me when I told them (with just a casual reference to my grandfather) that my information came from 'special powers; rather than that it had been obtained by tapping their rivals' Videophone line or from bribing a disaffected employee. (A practice, by the way, I frequently employ when... 'significant events occur beyond the range even of my widespread network'. It's good to have friends in distant camps).

Friends and colleagues who know I have been compiling, chapter by chapter, this account of a company's history have asked why I have restricted myself to the period when Hector Pennington was chairman; my personal involvement, they rightly say, goes back to his great-grandfather's time. My answer is twofold: one, I didn't have the communications technology in the previous two centuries that is available to me now; and, two, the company's progress was steady but relatively uneventful for most of its existence and it was only in Hector's time that we have had these outbreaks of passion and tragedy. It seems that technology and drama have come together.

I almost forgot: my name is Melvyn. It's an old Celtic name.

CHAPTER TWO

After telling you who I am, perhaps I should tell you where I am.

I live in the small town of Boskey Common (not to be confused with Boskey Village, a couple of miles away). It has been a long long time since there has been a common in these parts but the name still wafts up an image of a Hardyesque rural enclave miraculously preserved only fifteen miles from the centre of London; an image that is enhanced by the postal address being just inside the border of Hertfordshire. You will find it on John Speed's ancient maps where it is shown as Bossye and apparently much more important in those days than Colnesford, which now dominates the area.

Colnesford grew to prominence in the late nineteenth century through its brewing and printing industries, but these had declined almost to extinction by the 1980's when they were replaced by software-based service companies.

The road to London from Colnesford passes through Boskey Village then climbs the hill to Boskey Common before joining the A1. Around the turn of the nineteenth/twentieth centuries the two Boskeys housed a lively school of painting and attracted a colony of be-smocked aesthetes and craftpersons. Even at the time of these chronicles there were vestigial flutterings of artistic interests and impulses. But the artistic colony, too effete to foster vigorous growth, was succeeded by wave after wave of immigrants: first the coarse Londoners from the south-east; then the Asians, then the Jews, then the refugees from Eastern Europe and then the Chinese from Hong Kong; all following the direction taken by rags-to-riches generations in almost every metropolitan city: that is, from the east towards the north-west. At the time of this story it had been over half-a-century since an authentic Hertfordshire accent had been heard in Boskey Common.

Each immigrant wave brought with it its own package of skills, customs, shops, restaurants and religions. Kosher butchers flourished next to oriental vegetable-mongers on one side and purveyors of exotic spices on the other; until each in turn was engulfed by the mighty maw of the multistory supermarket which glowed and glittered where the church graveyard used to be. All Christian celebration had been brought together into the surpassingly ugly United Reform church half-way up the hill; the other centres of worship - Anglican, Catholic, Methodist, Baptist, etc. - had either been converted to or replaced by synagogues, mosques and temples of various types. I suppose one should take comfort in that the aura - if that is the appropriate term - of these ancient sites had been preserved, although no longer devoted to their original variety of god-head.

It was here in Boskey Common that Sir Arthur Pennington, Chairman and Chief Executive of the Extra Good(s) Co. Ltd., (also variously known as EGCol and ExGo) had both his home and his head office. His home was one of the few remaining early Regency villas in the High Street: it had a double-bow fronted elevation with sumptuously curved balustrades outlining its flat roof; and it was painted a rosy pink so that it blushed winsomely in the evening sun.

Earlier generations of his company's chairmen had run the business from offices in London, but the filth, discomfort and unreliability of public transport had so accelerated over the years - unlike its speed - that the capital's office blocks had been abandoned apart from a few dealing in shady travel businesses and louche entertainments. Transport had been improved beyond all measure when the cable cars were introduced but few companies could be persuaded to return to London again. Some brave souls had attempted to work from home but the joys and miseries of ambient domestic life had proved too distracting. Now every town and village had its own small business centres, often shared by a handful of people from half-a-dozen companies, where commercial empires on a national, even international, scale could be run via telecommunications networks.

EGCol had the top floor of one such centre on a site once occupied by a water company. It was hither that Sir Arthur Pennington used to travel a few hundred yards on his electric moped every morning to take control of his widely-distributed company And it was here that I reported every few weeks in my capacity as management adviser to the Chairman and Board.

One of my first tasks was to produce what was known as the company's 'mission'. I attempted to combined the traditional aspects of stated company objectives (I knew the Board would be uneasy if I left them out) with the features which were unique to EGCol. The version that was finally adopted was:-

The Extra Good(s) Company Ltd's objectives are:-

1) to survive

2) to buy, sell, distribute, market, deal, produce, manufacture and research into a range of goods and services without limit to their scope or nature except that they are undoubtedly and completely ethical in character; that is, for avoidance of doubt, that at no time in their history will they have been of physical, mental or spiritual pain, distress or discomfort to the human and animal kingdoms.

3) to foster long-term profitable growth.

The floor below EGCol housed Sir Charles Duke and his Tintagel Memento Co, (wholesaler of plastic piskies and related novelties to retail outlets in Cornwall).

Sir Arthur possessed many worthy qualities but abstention from strong liquors was not amongst them. Over-indulgence inevitably led him swiftly through the state of aggression to the even more repellent condition of maudlin tearfulness. One day, when I was alone with him in the EGCol offices, he shook his long wavy hair, blinked through his watery eyes and said he had a secret he must confide in someone and there was no-one around but me. I assumed an expression which combined receptivity and trustworthiness.

He tilted his great head towards me. "Did you know," he said, "that the one man I envy most in the world is sitting immediately beneath me?"

"Surely not!" I said. "Sir Charles Duke?"

"Got it in one."

"But... but... I thought you despised everything he does and stands for - plastic garden tat, unethical business practices..."

"I'm not talking about his business; I'm talking about his wife."

I was astonished. "Lady Iris?" I said. "You surprise me. I admit she's handsome... but she's such a cold fish."

"I wasn't contemplating a tumble in the hay," said Sir Arthur. "Anyway, my days of heaving and humping are over; too bloody athletic and sticky for me. Which, in a way, is my point. As you know I'm the third generation of Penningtons to run this business but I have no child of my own to take over from me and my lovely wife has long since passed away. I've considered the other Board members as possible successors, but none of them is leadership material. But then I think of Lady Iris: she has intelligence, determination and unbounded stamina - all balls-aching attributes in a wife (I wonder how old Charles puts up with her) but just what is needed in the mother of a captain of industry. Imagine combining all her masculine factors of intelligence and drive with my more feminine ones of intuition and imagination. The sprog would be a world-beater."

He paused for a moment and looked me squarely in the eyes. "I desire that marriage of qualities more than anything," he said deliberately.

"Are you putting this to me as a project?" I asked.

"Perhaps it's too much to expect."

"No, no, no, I'll see what I can do," I said hastily. (One has to show willing to please one's best clients, even when the means of doing so are none too clear).

I knew a little of Lady Iris's ancestry. She was the daughter of the Duke of Hertford's first marriage to Lady Blanche Colneford who had tragically died in a road accident on the A1. Lady Iris was the only product of that union, but it was known that the Duke had married again. Lady Iris's marriage to Sir Charles was without issue.

As it happened I ran into Sir Charles Duke on the way down on the escalator He was considering staging a conference of all his branch managers and asked my advice as to a suitable venue.

"In my experience," I said, "to be successful you need eyeball-to-eyeball contact for a considerable period without intervening opto-electronics."

"Is there such a place?"

"I've heard good things about Marion Island in the South Atlantic," I said. "It's one of the few places left in the world without an international switched holographic conference system. Otherwise the facilities at the conference centre are, I understand, first-class. And if you need a little light relief on the days you interrupt your conference to allow the secretaries to massage the minutes, you can have an expedition to watch the penguins mating. They tell me it combines eroticism with slapstick to an orgasmic degree."

"Sounds fun. I'll consider it."

That night Sir Charles informed his handsome but chilly wife that he was going to the South Atlantic for a week-long conference.

"That sounds dreary," said Lady Iris. "Would there be anything there to interest me?"

"Nothing. Unless you want to watch the merry antics of the penguins."

"God, no! You know how I hate wild life."

"Only too well," said Sir Charles.

They ruminated in silence. Then Sir Charles suddenly said: "I know: you could have a child. You've often said you would like one."

"Oh, really, Charles!" said Lady Iris. "That takes months and months!"

"I know you're fascinated by old customs and practices," said Sir Charles, "but there's no need to go to extremes. Use one of the new accelerated methods. There are lots on the market." Lady Iris accepted the proposition into her mind, cut it up into slices, carefully examined each slice, then put them together again.

"Good idea," she said. "I'll do it. It will help pass the time. We'll need to take out a dose from the sperm bank so don't forget to sign a withdrawal authorisation chit before you go."

The next morning I was passing the Duke's house just as Sir Charles was stepping into his personal cable-car.

"I've taken your advice," he said. "We're going to have our conference on Marion Island and I'm just off to the International Transport Centre."

He suddenly grimaced. "Oh, sod!" he shouted. "I intended to call in at the sperm bank to make a withdrawal but I don't have enough time."

"Have you got your authorisation with you?" I asked.

He dove into his pockets. "Yes."

"Well, let me have it and I'll get the dose for you and drop into your wife on my way home."

"Good man, you've saved my life."

"Not at all; it's a pleasure to be of service."

As soon as he had zoomed off I rushed round to the EGCol offices. Sir Arthur's massive body was slumped forward in his chair and his huge head was resting in his hands. He snorted gloomily when he saw me; he was still in black despond at his lack of an heir.

"Do you have your sperm bank chits here in the office?" I asked.

"What? Yes. Why?"

"Make out a withdrawal authorisation," I said, "and don't ask any questions."

Well, you can guess what I did. I went to the sperm bank, took out two vials of jollop, one in in Sir Arthur's name and one in Sir Charles', switched the labels and handed the Pennington one to Lady Iris that evening.

Three days after Sir Charles returned from his conference, Lady Duke was safely delivered of a healthy boy. Sir Charles was in raptures and even his wife's chiselled features occasionally warmed into a smile. And it was said that on that day a double rainbow was seen all over Hertfordshire and all the songbirds combined into one exultant chorus of jubilation.

But Sir Arthur Pennington was more miserable than ever. "It's bad enough not having a son of my own," he groaned, "but to hear my nearest rival boasting about his is more than I can bear."

"Cheer up, Sir Arthur," I said, "and prepare yourself for some good news."

One eye opened beneath a shaggy eyebrow. "Oh, what?"

I gave it to him straight from the shoulder. "That son of Lady Iris's isn't Charles Duke's at all. It's yours."

I then described my little ruse. For a moment the old man lay slumped in silence as the truth sunk in. Then he threw his head back in a great roar of delight, opened his arms as though to embrace the world and commenced to dance round the office, his huge legs stamping the floor like an elephant doing the zapadeado. It's a wonder he didn't go through to his cuckolded rival's office beneath.

Then, just as suddenly, he stopped dancing and flopped back into his chair with a moan.

"What's the matter now?" I asked, thinking my efforts had had but short reward.

"What's the good of the boy being mine," he groaned, "if he's being brought up as the son of someone else? Someone else will be playing with him, rearing him, educating him. I might never see him - and if I do it will only make me feel worse! I want him to succeed me in my business, not to that idiot Duke's." I conceded he had a point. I mumbled I would see what I could do.

Sad to say, Sir Charles's delight at the birth of his son (or, rather, the child he believed to be his son) was literally short-lived. On the tenth day after the baby's deliverance, he organised a 'wetting the baby's head' celebration in his club which culminated in his sampling every colour of the rainbow in the form of liqueurs. Feeling a little drowsy, he decided to go home early. On the way back in his cable-car, in order to shout his happiness to the town as it slid by underneath, he over-rode the safety mechanism of the car door and toppled to a multi-hued and aromatic death through the kitchen roof of a Chinese restaurant.

Both Sir Arthur and I attended his funeral at the multi-level crematorium. My greatest problem was preventing the old man from making ostentatious cow-eyes at the stately widow and from his bursting into chuckles as he thought of the demise of her late husband. As you would imagine, the ceremony was well-attended by relatives, friends, employees and representatives of organisations having a financial interest in the Tintagel Memento Co.; but one group stood out from the rest: three slender women, dressed from head to toe in black leather. I gathered that they were sisters and related in some way to Lady Iris and that their names were Morwaine, Elaine and Fay. Fay had been educated at a convent; I caught a glimpse of her austere white features through her veil and thought that I had never seen such an excoriating vision of beauty and depravity.

Sir Arthur allowed a proper period of mourning - seven days - to pass before paying court to the white-faced Lady Iris. He gave a presentation on the advantages that would accrue from their union: the merging of the two top floors of the tower block and of the integration of their communications centres, leading to saving in telecommunications links, computer costs and the rationalisation of management staff. How could a woman of Lady Iris's cast of mind resist such blandishments? After another week of careful thought (and access to data-bases giving Sir Arthur's personal fortune and business activities) she announced she was willing to marry again; but there was one over-riding consideration.

"What is that?" asked Sir Arthur.

"What of my little boy, Hector?" asked Lady Iris. "How will you relate to him?"

"I will cherish him as though he were my own son," promised Sir Arthur.

And so they were married at the Church of Divers Saints and Martyrs (the old United Reform) and their son, carried carefully in the arms of a Chinese maid at the rear of the church, chortled and chuckled to the delight of all who heard him.

CHAPTER THREE

That was the last chortling and chuckling to be heard from young Hector for many a long year. Even as a baby he preserved a solemn mien, neither laughing nor crying, gravely eating and drinking everything within reason that was put before him. By his third year he had already been fitted with contact lenses to counteract the eye-strain acquired in mastering the instructions of his virtual-reality construction set. He could handle multi-level transactions involving more than forty interfaces before he was able to walk, provided he was placed within reach of a work-station. By the age of seven he had devised a programme ('Satchmo') which could simulate trumpet solos and riffs that the real Armstrong had never got round to playing (a feat, as he informed his mother, far more difficult than replicating Russell's 'Principia Mathematica'). At twelve he had extracted the marrow from Shakespeare's tragedies and converted it into a single equation which could be used to generate new tragedies at will ('Sigmund, Prince of Austro-Hungary'; 'The Tragicall Historie of Herman Goering'; etc). By his late teens he was short-sighted, getting a little thin on top, hunch-shouldered, knock-kneed and the apple of his parents' eyes.

It was well that Sir Arthur took delight in his son because he derived little joy from other quarters. Although the office accommodation, the information technology and the staffs of his and Sir Charles Duke's old companies had been skillfully amalgamated, he was not reaping the success he had hoped for. This was not due to any shortfall in management skills, (after all, I was still his consultant), but to the increasing difficulty in identifying goods and services possessing the requisite ethical purity. Iron cooking pots for export to Matabeleland, for instance, were not only one of the company's most profitable lines, they were also held to meet the most high-minded desiderata; but it was then discovered, (by one of EGCol's rivals), that they had been fabricated from metal from old Challenger tanks. They were deemed as being imbued with the spirit of warfare and their distribution was halted - much to the annoyance of the Africans for whom they were intended. As another example, drugs capable of relieving the symptoms of beriberi were in heavy demand; but the company's Ethical Investigation Squad discovered they were based on the ejaculations of dolphins who had been stimulated, for that sole purpose, to the point of unbearable frustration. So their manufacture was ceased.

And so it went on. Nearly every product which seemed at first sight to manifest the high ideals of the Extra Good(s) Co. Ltd. revealed, upon examination, an unethical flaw which necessitated its deletion from the catalogue. Some Board members urged a relaxation from these impossibly high standards so as to preserve a permanent core of business activities which would at least keep the company's finances afloat. But Sir Arthur would have none of it. Whilst he was alive there would be no deviation from the principles that had characterised his company for three generations.

Meanwhile, I was developing my powers of observation-at-a-distance. I found I could scan what was occurring elsewhere by reflecting a powerful coherent laser beam from the Moon's surface back to Earth where it would interact with light waves from the object under scrutiny and so produce diffraction patterns which I could detect with a hypersensitive receiver It was not an entirely satisfactory method; in fact, to be frank, it was pretty awful. The Moon's surface is very uneven, so movement of my laser beam by as little as a fraction of a second of arc could deflect me from a fine piece of polished rock on to a non-reflecting area of volcanic ash. It was like combining advanced laser technology with the operating fumblings of a 1920's crystal set. Moreover, my receiver had to be immersed in liquid helium so that its own molecular agitation wouldn't swamp the tiny signals from the target; and liquid helium, as I found to my irritation, is not the easiest of substances to handle. There were times when I found it more reliable to guess - or, perhaps I should say, to divine - what was going on elsewhere rather than rely on my laser-tracker technology.

What I did gather, whether by technology or by ear-to-the-ground, was that all the directors and most of the managers of EGCol had become disenchanted with Sir Arthur Pennington and were plotting his overthrow. I didn't relish telling the old man myself so I called at his home one day when I knew he was at his office and broke the news to Lady Iris. She was now steely-haired and austere but as handsome as ever. She heard me in silence.

Then she said: "This is disgraceful. Is there anything you or I can do?"

"I don't think we can save Sir Arthur's position," I said, "but I have an idea as to how we can save the firm."

"Tell me."

"Not now. One shock at a time!" (Lady Iris was quite tough enough to receive two shocks in close sequence but I didn't want to dissipate the dramatic impact by running them together).

That evening, Lady Iris, without prevarication, told her husband that his colleagues were planning his downfall. The old man was deeply distressed.

"How could they!" he shouted. "How could they! After all that I have done for the company!"

"That's all very well," said Lady Iris, coolly, "but you must see it from their point of view. If the firm collapses so will their standards of living. You have got to do something to revive EGCol's fortunes."

The next morning Sir Arthur sent for his stores manager.

"How many of those iron cooking pots have we got in store?" he asked.

"About two thousand, sir."

"Are they still in reasonably good condition?"

"Oh, yes, sir. That's lovely metal, that is." (He didn't notice Sir Arthur's wince of disgust). "Not a spot of rust on them."

"Are they still wanted?"

"I believe so, sir. I heard the Sales Director say only the other day that the Africans were very upset when the delivery was cancelled."

"Get them out and packed. I'm going to take them to Matabeleland myself."

That evening Lady Iris tried to dissuade her husband from his mercy mission.

"I'm sure you mean well," she said, "but aren't you getting on a bit for this sort of heroic gesture? Can't one of the younger men go?"

"I'm sorry, my dear," said Sir Arthur, "but I've made up my mind. It's largely my fault that the family business has gone into decline so it's my responsibility to get it back on to an even keel. I won't be able to rest easy until I have taken some sort of positive action and this is something I can get stuck into immediately."

Next day, Sir Arthur, accompanied by two thousand iron cooking pots, took off from the travelport in a heavy duty cargo-ship. I tried to follow his progress on my laser-reflector system but it was maddeningly difficult keeping track of his supersonic craft as it roared across the Mediterranean into African skies. After an hour of intermittent flickering from my receiver I at last managed to find a good smooth reflecting area on the Moon and to receive a strong and steady signal as the ship sped along its course. And then the signal faltered, cut out.... and disappeared. I frantically re-tuned my receiver - nothing. I traced out a new pattern with my laser-beam on the Moon's surface, desperately seeking a more sensitive reflecting area.... still nothing.

Four days later the remains of the cargo-ship were found in the Rwandan jungle. The almost unrecognisable remains of an old white man were found inside; he had been pulverised to a pulp by ricocheting cooking pots. The reason for the disaster was never established.

Now, here's the strange thing. When I went round to the EGCol offices on the afternoon of the craft's disappearance I found that the company's entire communications and computer system - not only in Boskey Common, but nationwide - had gone out of action. Later, I compared the time of this incident, as reported in the control room log, with the official records of International Traffic Control and with my own loss of signal. They were identical. Sir Arthur and his company's nervous system had both crashed at precisely the same time.

Sir Arthur's carcass was massaged into an approximately humanoid shape and returned home. His company's directors put it about that the EGCol office had been closed down until the funeral as a mark of respect during a period of mourning. In fact they had been working furiously behind closed doors to revive the office information technology system, with total lack of success.

I accompanied Lady Iris to the crematorium. Although she was now seeing her second husband consigned to the furnace and, moreover, was aware that the family business was in deep trouble, she still retained her remarkable composure. That could not be said, I'm afraid, for those EGCol people who had snatched time away from the office to put in a token appearance at the funeral and whose cold perspiration indicated their mounting panic. The three tall sisters were there again, dressed, as before, entirely in black. When I glimpsed through her veil a flash of Fay's alabastine cruel beauty, my gizzards so writhed with lust I couldn't help uttering a sharp cry of anguish.

Lady Iris asked me to remain behind in her rose-tinted house after the other mourners had dipped into the finger buffet, quaffed her wine and left. She removed her veil, sat upright in a large armchair and looked me squarely in the face.

"Melvyn," she said, "I now have no-one to turn to but you. I trust I can depend upon your advice. What is to be done about the company?"

I made the usual remarks about how it was a privilege, nay, an honour, to serve her and then said "Send young Hector along and let him investigate the problem."

For a moment something approaching an expression of surprise tinged her features but she rapidly recovered from this unseemly display of emotion.

"Very good," she said, "I'll take him along tomorrow."

The staff at EGCol were naturally dismayed to have their panic-stricken remedial work interrupted by the stately Lady Iris and her weedy son. They were even more miffed when the lad sat at the console and played silent arpeggios on the keyboard whilst intently watching the display screen. After half-an-hour or so he just said "Right!", stood up and walked out, followed by his mother.

At Lady Iris's request I returned with him later that afternoon. He had with him a plug-in capsule containing a single crystal of which the molecular structure had been adjusted to act as an operating programme. He elbowed his way through the throng around the console, removed the standard capsule ('midst cries of "Hey, what d'you think you're doing?", "Take your hands off that!", "You've buggered up everything!", etc.,) and inserted his own. A few key-deflections and - Voila! - VDUs sprang into life, WPCs displayed uncorrupted text, printers started chattering and messages came pouring in from the far corners of the EGCol empire. The director responsible for information technology offered Hector a clammy hand. "That's very good, young man," he said. "Very impressive! How did you do it?"

"Before I tell you," said Hector. "I want to be made company communications manager."

"You want to be what!" spluttered the director, "That's quite out of the question. We already have a communications manager."

"But he hasn't been able to solve your problem," said Hector quietly. "I have."

"That's all very well," said the director, "but we can't displace him at a moment's notice. What on earth do you expect?"

Hector was silent for a few minutes, gazing at his module. Then, with a sigh, he pulled it out and put in in his pocket. Instantly, the printers ceased chattering, VDUs displayed chaotic garbage and the message streams dammed up. Hector, with me in tow, stalked out of the office.

We returned the next day at the same time and went through the same procedure, breathing electronic life into the office just as before. This time the director said "All right! You've made your point. I expect we can find a suitable post for you somewhere if you explain what's in the module."

"I don't want what you call 'a suitable post somewhere'," said

Hector. "I want to be a director."

"A director! But yesterday you said you wanted to be the communications manager!"

"That was yesterday. Today I want to be a company director."

"But you must know that that's impossible. Quite apart from it being unthinkable to have a teenager in such a responsible position, you must know that no new director appointments can be made until the chairman has been replaced."

Once again Hector unplugged his module and went home, leaving the company's communications in chaos.

I called on Lady Iris at her lovely home that evening. Hector had told her only the barest skeleton of the day's events so I filled in the details. Then I said: "I'm sure Hector will try again tomorrow and I think you should be there. But before that there's something very important you should know."

"Is this the second shock you warned me about?" asked Lady Iris. "If so I had better sit down and compose myself."

I was comforted by her slightly mocking tone. Lady Iris was not the sort to have a fit of the vapours about some item of fundamental family news.

"The revelation refers to your son, Hector," I said.

"What about him?"

"I have to tell you," I paused for dramatic effect... "he is not Sir Charles Duke's son but Sir Arthur Pennington's."

She gazed at me stonily. Her throat tautened and then relaxed again.

"Go on," she said.

I told her the whole story - Sir Arthur's admiration for her, his desire that she should be his son's mother, the spermicidal subterfuge, the fortuitous death of Sir Charles and the consequence that Hector's father and step-father were one and the same person.

Lady Iris accept this sensational news remarkably calmly.

"I see!" she said, after a moment's thought. "That explains a lot of things: such as my son being blonde like Sir Arthur and not dark and saturnine like Sir Charles; and the very close relationship that grew up between them. But what proof have you?"

I produced a dog-eared phial from my pocket. "This is labelled as being Sir Arthur's," I said, "but genetic analysis will show that it's Sir Charles's".

"Don't trouble," she said, "I'll take your word for it. I'll come with Hector to the office tomorrow at five o'clock. I'll see you then."

The directors, managers and staff were expecting us and had formed a semi-circle around the console. Hector slouched through the crowd, in bodily contrast to his stiffly upright black-gowned mother, and for the third time replaced the standard operating programme with his own. For the third time the office machinery came to life like Dr. Coppelius's toy-shop and messages illuminated the VDUs.

"Hector," said the director ingratiatingly, "do be reasonable. I, and my fellow directors, acknowledge that you have solved a problem that has completely baffled us; but is there any need to be so possessive about it? Don't you realise that as well as the entire company's your mother's well-being is at stake?"

"I'm prepared to let you have my module," said Hector, flatly, "but only if I'm made Chairman."

"Chairman! That's more ridiculous than ever! Lady Iris, can't you make him see sense? Won't you impress on him that only a Pennington can be Chairman of the company? Actually we have traced a distant relation but he lives in Tasmania and it will be several days before he gets here."

Lady Iris rose to her feet. The half-circle of EGCol employees were silenced by her silvery charisma.

"All of you listen to me very carefully," she declaimed.

"Hector, my beloved Hector, was not only brought up by my late husband, Sir Arthur Pennington, as though he were his own son - he was his own son! It was Melvyn here who engineered this happy arrangement and he will tell you the details when I leave you in a few minutes time. Now, speaking as the next-of-kin of my late husband

and therefore as Chairman-regent, I make this formal announcement: Hector is the legitimate heir to Sir Arthur Pennington and from this day forth he is Chairman of the Extra Good(s) Company!"

She turned and left the office, leaving the meeting silent and still, as though hypnotised. Before they had time to recover I hobbled into the centre of the group and launched into my account of the swapped fatherhood. (There were murmured insinuations that I had been seen in the computer room in recent weeks and might have been the cause of their troubles, but I treated these calumnies with the contempt they deserved). When I had finished, Hector stood up and swept the arc of onlookers through his glinting contact lenses.

"I will be holding a meeting in the car-park of the King Charles Recreational and Instructional Gardens at 10 am on Sunday morning," he proclaimed, "and I want you all to be there."

CHAPTER FOUR

It was a splendid sight that Sunday morning in Charlies Fields (as the King Charles Recreational and Instructional Fields were known) with the men in their quartered tabards and pied tights and the women in their waist and shoulder ribbons and sequined wimples. Hector and Lady Iris had persuaded the leaders of all the Boskey Common religious communities to be present; even in that colourful crowd they stood out in their embroidered cloaks and bejewelled crowns (the Anglican vicar and the RC priest were a little late, it being a Sunday). Nor had the Chairmen and Chief Executives of other local business empires been forgotten; they strode with dignity through the throng wearing the sashes and chevrons betokening their august offices. Overhead the multi-coloured cable-cars swished to the Charlies terminal bringing more and more citizens to join the multitude.

I saw a woman who looked familiar sitting near the edge of the dais. "Who's that?" I asked Lady Iris.

"That's Morwaine," replied her ladyship. "She's a relative of mine."

"Oh, of course," I said. "I couldn't place her because I have only seen her in mourning weeds. What is she doing here?"

"She has brought her son, Jasper, with her. He's the possible contender for the chairmanship that the EGCol directors referred to yesterday (although if they knew anything about my family they should know he's not a true Pennington at all).

"Morwaine sent him to one of those rough tough finishing schools in Tasmania but she fetched him back when she heard the chairmanship might be vacant. They must both be very disappointed."

"Oh, yes, I can see him now." (I had spotted a sallow youth with a long pustular face, droopy bloodless lips and spiky hair). "He seems very young."

"Yes, he's only twelve. He should be no threat to Hector."

I thought I felt a sudden shaft of cold air penetrate my cloak and go through to my bones. "No, no!" I said, hesitantly. "Of course not!"

Hector mounted the dais and clipped on his lapel microphone. Silence rippled out from the stage to the furthest periphery of the crowd. He spoke. It couldn't be said his voice was pleasant: it had a harsh metallic quality and varied very little in amplitude or tone; yet it was curiously compelling, demanding focussed attention. He showed no signs of nervousness.

"I'm very glad you have all found time to come here this morning," he began, "because it gives me a unique opportunity to proclaim my business philosophy and to outline my plans for the future. I am also glad to be addressing those of you who are still at home and watching this event on Cable TV.

"As most of you know, my beloved father, Sir Arthur Pennington, died in tragic circumstances two weeks ago; and I, his undisputed heir" [did I detect sharp glances between the Ladies Iris and Morwaine?] "have taken over the chairmanship of the Extra Good(s) Company Ltd. I know there are those who think I am too young and inexperienced to play such an important role. I must acknowledge I am lacking in years and hitherto have not taken much part in the company's day-to-day business. But I come from a long line of Penningtons and the company ethos is in my blood. As to my policies, I declare before you I will not depart from the company's traditional principles; indeed, I will reiterate them here and now. You can depend that whilst I am Chairman, EGCol will seek out, support and promote goods and services - and only those goods and services - that will be for the benefit of mankind and the environment. We will not participate in any activity just for mercenary reasons; we will not toady for the favours of the media or the establishment; we will not discriminate between sexes, colours, creeds, castes, age groups or even species. Our slogan will be: 'In Deed to Goodness!'

"I know this won't be easy. I am well aware the company has been faltering in its attempt to operate within the confines of these high ideals. But I am confident that if we apply ourselves with clear minds and pure hearts then we will not only be successful financially but we will also end our work each day glowing with the warmth that job satisfaction can bring." [Applause from citizens; mocking expressions and raised eyebrows from EGCol staff].

"What I have said so far is for the ears of all you good people of Boskey Common; you have the right to know the objectives of one of the biggest enterprises in your community What I have to say now is addressed principally to the directors, managers and staff of the company. I - we - cannot afford to have halfheartedness in application to duty, over-fastidiousness in our observance of nominal working hours or a cynical attitude to our ethical modes of conduct. Since I don't know you all personally, I am unable to decide immediately which of you will meet these requirements and so be able to stay with the company and which of you will be advised to seek employment elsewhere. Therefore, to be consistent and fair, I am here and now dismissing every one of you" [Gasps! Cries of No! No!] "yes, I repeat, dismissing every one of you and then I will interview, as rapidly as I can, those of you who wish to apply for your old positions.

"Thank you again for your attention. Enjoy your day."

Hector clambered down from the dais and came to join Lady Iris and me. The public began to disperse, leaving knots of EGCol staff in animated discussion and sending many a shaft of angry glances at their new young master.

"Very well done, my dear," said Lady Iris. "Beautifully said."

"Yes, er, congratulations," I joined in. "Good show. I must say the idea of sacking everyone and then re-engaging only those you really want is quite ingenious. Very bold; gets rid of the old dead wood. Have you consulted the unions?"

"The local conveners automatically get sacked as well."

"Yes, of course. The trouble is - if I may say so - this bold action leaves you and the company very vulnerable during the transitional period in which you are building up your new establishment."

"Vulnerable to what?"

"Take-over bids... security breaches... poaching of your best staff (those you don't wish to get rid of)... price undercutting..."

"All right, there's no need to go on. I hope I can take it for granted that you will advise me on these matters just as you did for my father and his father before him?"

"Of course. You can count on my loyalty."

"Thanks. Well, what shall we do to protect ourselves during what you call the transitional period?"

"Make your first appointment. In my view the most important of all is your Finance Director. It is his skill and integrity more than any other's that you have to depend upon in your early years."

"Who is the present Finance Director?" asked Hector.

Lady Iris leaned forward. "A Mr Keith Kendall. A very sound man."

Hector was shocked. "Kendall! Oh, I know who you mean. But he's terribly old - he's nearly forty! His knowledge of parallel processing is virtually nil!"

"Neverless," I said, "he has the advantage of being in position, so we should give him serious consideration. I can tell you that he joined the company as a young man, straight from college. He was placed in the Accounts Department, checking monies received against issued invoices. He was so assiduous in settling bad debts that he came to the notice of your father who supported him in obtaining his professional qualifications. He has been with the company for over twenty years and there is not a facet of its work with which he is not familiar. That's him over there." I pointed to a tall thin man in subfusc clothes standing amongst a group of EGCol employees - or perhaps I should say 'ex-employees'.

"And his loyalty?"

"Beyond all question."

"It's about to be questioned at any moment," said Lady Iris.

She had noticed Morwaine and Jasper sidling their way towards where Kendall was in deep discussion. I grabbed Hector by the hand and hustled him through some hostile by-standers to where Kendall, unaware of impending rival bids for his services, was chatting to his colleagues. As we whisked him away to the bowling green pavilion, the quietest place in the fields, I could sense Morwaine's glance of frustrated fury directed at Lady Iris and me. There and then, in that echoing wooden pavilion, we uttered a verbal contract reinstating Kendall to his former position, much to his flustered delight.

EGCol's Board Room on Monday morning looked disturbingly deserted. Hector's slight figure was slumped at one end of the huge oval table with Kendall seated close by his right hand. I, knowing my place as a mere adviser, sat a few places away. The remaining ten places were empty; no other directors had yet been appointed. Hector turned to me.

"Melvyn," he said, "yesterday you forecast that the company would be vulnerable to attack from outside forces during this sensitive period. I can well believe there will be many people who will think I am green in the ways of business and too inexperienced to handle hostile approaches. But do you have any firm information about unfriendly action?"

"I have, Chairman, I have." I said. "A group I am calling the Hadrian Consortium is planning an attack."

"What is the Hadrian Consortium?"

"It's a group of eleven companies located geographically on a line from Carlisle to Newcastle, roughly along the route of Hadrian's Wall. They have, in the past, specialised in supplying simple items of equipment to the Third World - well-pumps, rice-boilers, satellite terminals, that sort of thing. Unfortunately, the Third World depends on grants from the World Bank to make these purchases and the Bank discovered that the goods supplied by the Hadrian group were shoddy and did not meet their specifications; consequently, the Hadrian Consortium has been struck off the list of approved suppliers. They have been struggling to make their way back into this trade area for the last eighteen months; they are well aware that the World Bank respects EGCol as an honest upright company, so they believe that if you could recruit some of the key people you sacked yesterday, the Bank would be so impressed by this infusion of talent and dependability that supply approval would be restored. They are setting up a recruiting centre in Retching Heath which will be in full swing by tomorrow evening."

"The devils! But how do you know all this?"

"I arranged for the nearest EGCol company units in the Hadrian area to tap their communication lines and send the information to me."

"But... but... that's quite unacceptable! It's totally unethical! I gave a public assurance only yesterday that this would be a wholly ethical company."

"Forgive me, Chairman, but the undertaking you gave was that all the goods and services provided by the company would be ethical. You didn't say anything about the company's business methods."

"That's splitting hairs. I find your action distasteful."

"Sir, we must be practical. We can't be a successful trading company in the face of uninhibited competition unless we use the devils' weapons."

Hector sat chewing his lip, plainly disturbed by my robust methods. Fortunately it didn't occur to him to ask why I had specified the Hadrian area to be tapped - after all, the attack could have come from anywhere. I had made no such specification - I had instructed every EGCol office, no matter where they were, to tap as many local companies as they could.

Eventually he spoke. "Very well," he said. "I suppose I must - but with reluctance - act upon the information you have placed before me; but I must say I am greatly upset to have to depend upon such underhand methods on my very first day in office.

"What do we do to counteract this recruiting drive?"

"We must arrange that only those people you can afford to lose turn up for the interview."

"And how do we do that?"

"We get Kendall here to write out a list of people who we most wish to retain - the most competent, imaginative and loyal."

Kendall looked alarmed. "Oh, I couldn't possibly do that. I don't wish to sit in judgment on my colleagues."

"Oh, yes you can!" I said firmly. "Don't forget the Chairman has especially honoured you by making you his first directorial appointment. You were seen as crucial to setting the company on its feet."

Kendall blushed and muttered something under his breath; he then bowed his head over his pad and started tapping on his keyboard.

"When we have compiled our list of favoured people, what then?" asked Hector.

"The recruiting programme tomorrow evening," I said, "will take place in the upstairs meeting room at 'The Three Dunlops' in Retching Heath. I suggest we go along there at lunchtime today and have a few drinks. One of us - me - will slip upstairs and use their fax machine to sent out some messages, supposedly coming from the Hadrian team. The messages will be delivered to all the people on Kendall's list, telling them the recruiting session has been cancelled, at least for them. Then, if they meet one of their colleagues who has been invited to the interview they will think they have been spurned for some reason. In this way the Hadrian team will pick up only the duds and you will offer posts to the good'uns."

Hector had gone broody again. "I don't like this," he muttered, "I don't like this at all."

"I haven't finished yet," I said. "You might as well have all my unappealing proposals at once."

I turned to Kendall. "What about the Hadrian companies?" I asked. "Do they have any good senior people, people who would be a credit to EGCol?"

"Why, yes," he said. "They have two or three. Frankly I have always felt they were out of place in such questionable companies."

"What's in your dark and twisted mind, Melvyn?" asked Hector apprehensively.

"I propose, Chairman, that we should launch a counter-attack."

"A counter-attack?"

"Precisely. This is a classic battle situation. The enemy prepares to attack. We, the innocent party, glean from our intelligence that the assault is about to take place and prepare our defences. (That's the stage we have reached in our discussions so far). We now try to turn the tables by closing in on the enemy's base whilst his high command is down south attacking us."

"Be more specific."

"Right. Whilst the cream of the Hadrian Consortium's managing and personnel directors are on our doorstep in Retching Heath, we move smartly up to Gateshead and make a counter bid for their best people."

"Melvyn, you are going too far!"

"I don't think so. We can get there by cable-car in three hours."

"I didn't mean that and you know it. I mean that you are adopting the underhand means employed by our rivals."

"Ah, but unlike them, we are doing so for the best possible motives!" I replied with sweet reasonableness. "I'm sure that the great and good Hadrian people who Kendall will identify for us will only be too delighted to leave companies whose honour has been blotted by being struck off the World Bank list. Instead, they will be invited to join a company - our company - whose name is a by-word for the goodness of its goods and the serviceability of its services... particularly as we will be offering them 25 per cent more money."

Hector made every show of distaste but eventually consented to my little plan. Kendall drew up two lists: one, the EGCol people we wished to retain; and two, much shorter, the people we wished to poach from the north.

And so it came to pass. We did go to 'The Three Dunlops' that day and send out dis-inviting faxes to our chosen ones; and we did shoot up to Gateshead and pick up two very promising senior executives for ourselves.

The next week they joined us round the great oval table: Lance Mere became our Managing Director and James Perceval our Director of Engineering.

CHAPTER FIVE

Although dismayed at the thought of losing the companionship of her only son, Lady Iris recognised that now he had reached the age of eighteen, and was a company chairman to boot, it was time he had an establishment of his own. After a few hours browsing through the interactive picturedata frames on the CableTV real estate channel she located a suitably prestigious executive residential development on the fringe of Edgemore Heath, just a kilometre away from Boskey Common. It comprised a central utility tower containing all the essential features (elevators, plumbing, environmental control, communications and power wiring, etc.) into which living, sleeping, entertainment, cooking and hygiene space units could be plugged as required. The local cable-car network was connected by drop wires straight to the topmost platform where Hector's private plum-coloured cable carriage could be stabled when not in use. All deliveries - parcels, furniture, fuel and comestibles - were conveyed through subterranean pneumatic tubes into the basement dispatch room, adjacent to the centre for the electronic distribution of mail, fax, television, telephony, local news services and remote conference facilities. Lady Iris was impressed but decided not to move in with Hector but to remain alone in her rose-coloured Regency villa.

During the confusion caused by Hector's moving home and whilst the EGCol office was still sparsely attended, I installed a new supervisory and security system which embraced all the Pennington domiciliary and business centres. I employed a cellular microwave system working at 90Ghz; it was by no means ideal - radio at these wavelengths suffers badly from precipitation attenuation and multipath reflections - but by using path triangulation and some pretty sophisticated nodal switching I generally managed to get usable sight and sound from the more interesting locations.

When he had overcome the trauma of moving home, Hector called a meeting of his skeleton Board of Directors.

"Ultimately" he said, "I intend that our company will identify itself with a massive and serious project which will be recognised throughout the world as of outstanding benefit to mankind - not of mere material benefit but of spiritual value as well. It will be, if you will, our Grail. But meantime we need to build up our expertise, our staff and our physical management facilities by undertaking a project which, although undoubtedly ethical in character is not demanding in scale. Any suggestions?"

Keith Kendall, Director of Finance, spoke. "I wonder if I may put forward a proposal," he said timidly. "It's an idea that occurred to me a few weeks ago but I've never had the opportunity before now of having it taken seriously. I am always appalled - as I'm sure we all are - by the scenes we see so often on television of the widespread starvation in large areas of Africa, South America and the Indian sub-Continent. Millions of people are wholly dependent on the local crops: when the harvest is good, they subsist on a monotonous diet of rice or mealie-flour; when it is poor - which is more often than not - they have nothing at all. What these people need is a diet of good solid protein coming from a source of supply they can depend upon, year in, year out."

He paused; his eyes gleamed. "Go on," Hector encouraged.

"Quite by chance," Kendall continued, "I saw a television documentary a few weeks ago about the Indians of the Amazon rain forest. And do you know what one particular tribe lives on?... dried tadpoles! And then it struck me: what could be easier than farming tadpoles? Frogspawn is produced in Nature in superabundance and survives every variation of the English winter climate. We can deposit spawn in large tanks and ensure that their liquid environment possesses every nutrient needed for a heavy crop of tadpoles. Then - just before they have developed too far frogwise - they are lifted out by mechanically-operated meshes, slid into huge microwave ovens and then dried until they are nicely crisp and golden-brown. We then have a product rich in protein, small in volume and light in weight which can readily be packaged and transported to almost anywhere in the world. We will, of course, allow a small percentage to develop to full frog status so that we can generate enough spawn for the next cycle; and those, having performed their generative function, can either be exported to France or we might even start a fashion for fast-frog eateries in Britain."

"Looks interesting at first sight," said Hector. "Does everyone agree that the idea merits further consideration? Any dissension? No? Well, thank you, Kendall; please produce a fully-quantified business plan and bring it back to the Board in four weeks' time."

Kendall's presentation to the Board on the appointed day was well received. James Perceval had produced conceptual designs and preliminary costings of the great meshes and the microwave oven towers and Kendall had received assurance from the Ministry of Overseas Development and Export (MODEX) that start-up funding would be forthcoming for such a commendable project. Lance Mere, the Managing Director, was convinced there would be ample facilities for the hardware production in the many disused aircraft factories in that part of Hertfordshire. According to Kendall's spread-sheet, the project should break even in five years and be soaring into profit in six-and-a-half. The Board gave formal approval for the scheme to go ahead and to commence the recruitment of the scores of designers, software engineers and progress chasers who would be needed.

Morale soared. The first major project under the new management was under way! Hector, however, had some private reservations. He had been badly alarmed by the attack from the Hadrian consortium and asked me whether they were likely to harry him again; he was at a critical stage of establishing public esteem.

"Don't worry," I assured him. "The Hadrian companies will themselves be the objects of hostile bids from a group of Middle Eastern firms and there will be protracted and expensive legal battles. You will have nothing to fear from them for three years at least."

I was strictly correct in asserting there were no discernible threats from outside the company; there were, however, some internal problems. One of EGCol's sub-contractors, Timbertops of Dromdeal, which was to provide the enormous frames for the tadpole-lifting meshes, had run into cash-flow difficulties and was being threatened with closure by the banks. Hector went in person to see its chairman, Leo Gance, and arranged all the support that was needed from his own private fortune and by diversion from the MODEX grants. Leo was, of course, duly grateful and ingenuously introduced Hector to his daughter, Gwendoline, a comely girl of nineteen. A fusion of EGCol and Timbertops, he argued, would augment the unsurpassed creative talents of EGCol with the outstanding production capabilities of Timbertops. How better to cement such a relationship than by Hector marrying Gwendoline?

Hector consulted his mother upon his return. Lady Iris subjected the proposal to her usual cool scrutiny.

"There's a lot to be said for it," she said. "It would make good business sense. And it's about time you were married. What is she like, this Gwendoline girl?"

Hector was disconcerted by the question; he tried to remember back to his meeting with his potential wife.

"Oh, I don't know," he said. "She seemed all right."

So it was agreed that Hector would marry Gwendoline and that they would live together in his new dwelling which he henceforth named Dromdeal Tower to make his bride feel at home. A few days before the wedding she moved to Boskey Common and stayed in rented rooms in 'The Hole-Diggers Arms'. She visited Hector several times to discuss the detailed arrangements for the forthcoming nuptials.

"You do realise," she said on one occasion, "that the whole point of marriage is to have children? It's particularly important in our case because we need family continuity in cementing our companies together."

"That's a point," said Hector. "I must admit I hadn't given it much thought. I'll have to produce a few emissions of semen and lodge them with the Edgemore Offspring Production Unit for amalgamation with your ova."

"Oh, no! I don't want that!" protested Gwendoline. "I want to do things properly, like they did in the old days. I'm a romantic."

"A romantic! What do you mean by that?"

"Well, I want us to couple together physically. I want carnal congress."

"Do you mean like...? Good God, that's disgustingly messy! That's absolutely revolting!"

"Well, that's what I want. And unless we celebrate our union like they did when Britain was great and had an empire, the wedding is off!"

Hector, as always, referred back to his mother.

"My goodness!" she said. "She must be a primitive little hoyden! I must admit that that's what I had in mind when you were first being planned but my first husband soon convinced me that that sweaty wrestling form of intimacy was frightfully out of date. So she wants to go back to it, does she? I suppose this is the sort of thing one has to put up with if one marries someone from the provinces. I have to tell you, Hector, I have no first-hand experience of such practices; as I have said, I was deterred from employing them. But I believe some of the more authoritative manuals on the subject have been transferred to video disc."

So Hector, like his parents before him was married at The Divers Saints and Martyrs and there was a magnificent reception in Lady Iris's lovely rosy home. All the wit and beauty and the great and the good of Boskey Common were there, together with the senior strata of EGCol's staff. The three sisters were there, too, radiant in their fluorescent yellow and orange ribbons. Morwaine had brought her sulky son, Jasper, glowering through his pimples; Elaine's pre-pubescent daughter, Leonora, was there, too; Fay, of course, was unmarried and childless... and liquefied my gizzards each time she unleashed on me her icy Beardleyesque smile. After we had all ingested the festive fare and laughed at the witty speeches, the happy couple drove off in a splendid old Mazda to Dromdeal Tower. Cheering throngs lined the streets: many of them had not seen a surface vehicle for fifteen years or more.

Hector needed a good few stiff drinks that night to suppress his inhibitions; even so, he was still gauche with shyness when he led his bride by the hand up to his brilliant new bedroom. She showed no such reserve; she glided into the bathroom and soon re-appeared wearing nothing but a translucent red waist-slip. Hector gazed in wonder at her voluptuous spacial modulations.

"Aren't you going to take your clothes off?" she demanded brusquely, giving him a sharp shove on his shoulder.

"Is that really necessary?"

"Of course it's necessary! You can't enjoy romantic union unless you feel the warmth of leg upon-leg, body upon body, flesh upon flesh!"

Hector shuddered in distaste and reluctantly wriggled out of his tabard and under-vest. Gwendoline stared in mounting disgust as his twisted puny rib-cage was gradually revealed.

But, gallant trouper that she was, she pressed on.

"Come on!" she cried. "Now your boots and tights!"

Hector turned away, choking with embarrassment.

Gwendoline could scarcely suppress her cry of disappointment at the sight of his flaccid buttocks and legs like early-season celery. She turned him round and stared sternly at his shrinking figure.

"Haven't you prepared for tonight?" she demanded roughly.

"Of course I have!" said Hector, offended at this rude treatment. "I have ordered a laser video disc to be switched through from the central video library."

"You've ordered a video on our wedding night! What on earth is it?"

"It's called 'The Best of the Perfumed Garden'".

"Good grief! Are we going to perform step-by-step instructions?"

"Not necessarily. It's an interactive video, so we can always stop it and run through it frame by frame if we lose the thread of whatever it is we're supposed to be doing."

"For goodness sake! Well, if that's that way things are going to be, switch on the wretched TV and select your disc."

She jumped on the bed and pulled him roughly beside her. They flailed around for a few minutes.

"Wait a moment!" yelled Hector. "I can't see the screen. My contact lenses have steamed up."

He dropped off the end of the bed and crawled across the floor to drag the TV closer. There were shots of waving palm-trees and an oleaginous voice, after a short introduction, began describing various forms of congress, athletically illustrated by a couple of writhing copper-coloured bodies.

"There's a control pad on your side of the bed," shouted Hector above the farmyard sounds. "Press the reverse button. I want to see that bit again."

"Right! I've pressed the bloody button! Are you just going to watch or are you going to get into the action?"

"I'm doing my best. Look, your left leg has to go over there and my right arm has to... oh, it's no good, I can't see. Your chest is obscuring the screen."

"My chest, as you call it, is supposed to cause you paroxysms of delight, not be elbowed off to one side!"

Hector wriggled to another position.

"Aha, we've got the hang of it now," he cried. We're making the right lamb-bleating noises. Now, put your right thigh under my left armpit..."

"You've switched to the wrong track, you idiot!" shouted Gwendoline. "These are the instructions for a tall thin woman and a short fat man!"

But they persisted and after a further fifteen minutes or so they lay back on the crumpled bed-clothes, breathing heavily.

"How was it for you?" asked Gwendoline sarcastically, furious with frustration.

"I quite liked the last bit," smiled Hector in all innocence.

"God save us all!" snapped Gwendoline.

Although far from attaining Olympic standards as a lover - indeed, he scarcely merited prep-school sports-day rating - Hector began to enjoy this primitive form of gender coupling and demanded his conjugal rights from Gwendoline as often as once a week. Gwendoline, however, was far from satisfied by these sessions (which she likened to her friends as being raped by a stick-insect) and would lie planning the new bedroom curtains whilst Hector's raptures were in progress. Hector began to sense that the warmth of their relationship - which was never equatorial - was beginning to cool and sought conquests elsewhere.

He happened to call upon his mother one weekend when the lovely Elaine and her daughter, Leonora, were visiting. Unusually, he was deaf to Lady Iris's wit and wisdom; his eyes were flickering from Elaine to Leonora, from Leonora to Elaine, wondering who was the more desirable. Pretending to be keen on educating them into the principles and procedures of his company, he invited them to join him at the EGCol offices which, he said, could be appreciated more readily whilst the staff was away. As he led them into his own office he felt his pulse thumping and his tights succumbing to increasing tumescent pressure. His mind went into binary mode... mother? daughter? mother? daughter?... Suddenly impulsively, he thrust a set of tadpole mesh plans into Leonora's hands to keep her amused, pushed her into Kendall's empty office and then flung Elaine onto his big black leather couch before she had time to express her astonishment. All I could see on my supervisory system was a cloud of multi-coloured ribbons and shifts.

I slept very badly for the next few nights. I had dream after dream in which Hector - my charge - wandered in delightful gardens, smelling the flowers,... and was then stung by a deadly serpent; or rode on horseback to a pretty village, stopping at the inn for jug of ale, then fell to the ground clutching at his scorching throat; or drifted down a river on a punt, the sunlight through the willow fronds dappling the water, only to tip screaming over the weir...

I visited Lady Iris to give her my monthly report on the company's progress. When I had finished I gradually worked the conversation round to the three lovely sisters, Morwaine, Elaine and Fay.

"It was such a delight seeing them at Hector's wedding." I said. "Previously I had only met them at funerals, swathed in veils and black clothes. They really are very beautiful."

"Yes," Lady Iris agreed, "Elaine and Morwaine have always been greatly admired. Fay is rather too intense and intellectual to be appreciated by men. Did you know it was she who gave Hector the computer module that put EGCol back into action when my dear husband died?"

"No!"

"She did. And she has threatened to take it back again if the company, or Hector, do not comport themselves to her satisfaction."

"Extraordinary! You have often referred to them in casual conversation merely as your 'relatives'. Might I ask what is the precise relationship?"

"Well, you probably know that I am the only daughter of the Duke of Hertfordshire's first marriage, to Lady Blanche Colneford." I nodded. "After her tragic death, my father married again to Lady Florence Edgemore. Morwaine, Elaine and Fay are the daughters of that second marriage,"

"So they are your half-sisters rather than - as so many people imagine - your cousins?"

"I suppose they are."

On the occasion of the next EGCol Board meeting I asked to speak to Hector alone after the formal items had been concluded. "I'm busy." he said. "Don't take too long."

"Trust me, I won't" I said. "Because you are going to get very angry with me and I will need to leave your presence as soon as possible."

"What's this all about?"

"I believe..." I stammered. "I believe... Oh, God, how can I put this?... I believe you have been having a close relationship with Lady Elaine."

He was furious. He grasped me by the neck of my tabard. He was only a little fellow but anger had strengthened his grip.

"How do you know all this? Have you been spying on me?"

"You know me, sir!" I spluttered. "You know me! I have these special gifts! I can see across time and distance. I have prophetical dreams!"

"Well, if I have been seeing Elaine, what of it?"

"Oh, sir, sir!" I gasped. "Only bad will come of it. You have been shagging your auntie!"

CHAPTER SIX

Hector spent the next few months building up his staff, appointing new directors and revivifying those projects which had been active during his father's time and which had the potential of being both beneficial to mankind and profitable for the company. In all these activities he came to rely upon the sturdy unflagging support of the greatest prize of his northern conquest, namely Lance Mere, his Managing Director. Lance was not the most imaginative of men but he was an excellent organiser and admirable in putting into effect the ideas of others. It was he who introduced Mark Cornwall to Hector as a possible Director of Marketing.

Mark, as his name suggested, was a Westcountryman. He had previously headed the marketing department of an educational toy manufacturer which had unfortunately collapsed because the children had shown no interest in its products. This had been no fault of Mark's, who had laboured mightily, employing every device known to the marketing world to boost sales; but the children had resolutely turned away from anything that had an aura of 'doing good' about it. A lesser man in Mark's position would have been tempted to urge his company to turn to producing miniature weapons of mass destruction which have been so popular with young folk through the ages. But Mark resisted this easy solution; which was why Hector had felt drawn towards him and probably why his old firm had gone bust.

So Mark joined Lance Mere, Keith Kendall and James Percival - and, of course, Hector - round the great oval table and was soon imbued with the heady spirit of entrepreneurial drive combined with the essence of benevolence which characterised our company. He was invited by the Board to draw up a portfolio of goods and services which would bring in an early positive cash flow and maintain long-term profitable growth. It was appreciated that this was not an undertaking that could be carried out overnight. Having reviewed the range of work done by the old pre-Hector EGCol, Mark selected a few projects which might be resuscitated fairly easily because all the production tools, patterns, mandrels and software for computer-aided design and manufacture were still available. (One such old favourite was the cast iron cooking pot, but this was not pursued on account of its melancholy family associations). The first to be brought back into life was the transparent paving slab.

As one of the requirements of the Great Transport Act, which had virtually abolished all passenger road transport and replaced it by cable-car system, the structure of pavements had been radically re-defined. In the previous decades, more and more services - electricity, water, sewage, gas, telecommunications, cable TV - had been buried underground in the asphalt pavements. When a new service was introduced, or an old one augmented, the pavements had to be hacked up, usually by hand, then re-instated when the new ducts or cables had been laid; and if faults occurred experimental holes had to be dug in order to locate them. The result was an uneven, unsightly and dangerous walking surface in a state of constant upheaval.

The great Transport Act changed all that. Solid pavements were replaced by a series of chambers, two or three metres deep, equipped with racking and brackets on which various ducts and cables could be laid. The ground-level surface comprised square slabs laid on a standard grid, which could be readily lifted when access for new work or maintenance was required and then dropped back into place and locked in position when the work was completed. EGCol had been one of the many companies to have joined in the re-paving of Britain back in the early days of this great reform. Its subsequent novel contribution - which had reached advance design stage but never implemented - was to make the square slabs of transparent material and the items underneath a delight to behold. The first stage was to paint the ducts in bright colours, each appropriate to its function (electricity - red, water - blue, sewage - brown, and so on). This was not only visually attractive, it assisted the maintenance teams rapidly to identify their own plant. The next stage was to realise that any empty space below ground level would inevitably become waterlogged and then to exploit that fact. To that end, the EGCol ecology department had designed a pattern of waterlilies, ferns, oxygenating weeds and multi-coloured fish which would delight the perambulating spectators above.

Mark decided to put these designs into effect and persuaded James Percival's engineering department to set out a few streets of Boskey Common with transparent pavements at EGCol's expense. He then invited counsellors from all over Hertfordshire to visit the site of the trial. They were delighted. Orders for major installations first trickled and then flowed in in mighty volume. It was a classic EGCol venture: the transparent slabs were of toughened glass, which, derived as it is from sand, is almost inexhaustible in availability; the frames were of steel, re-cycled from the matrices of demolished reinforced concrete buildings; and the result was undoubtedly an enhancement of the environment.

Mark's next resuscitation from EGCol's portfolio was the electronic garden. Although most citizens (apart from the wealthy, like the Penningtons) lived in multi-storey apartment blocks with no more access to flora and foliage than could be afforded by a window-box, many had atavistic desires to have a garden which could be admired from their windows and perhaps even entered into from time to time. The desire to indulge in the physical aspects of gardening - digging, weeding, pruning, compost-turning - had, however, atrophied. An earlier generation of EGCol R&D staff had recognised how technology could satisfy this wish for the great outdoors by employing television projection tubes to display high definition pictures on large screens placed outside the apartment's windows. Gardens could then be planned and constructed simply by feeding instructions into the picture generator: perhaps a flowering cherry in mid-lawn, rambling roses over olde-worlde-out-buildings, a clump of lupins here, a bunch of violets there, and, maybe, the odd delightful pond or two. Of course, there was no need for the electronic gardeners to confine themselves only to those plants that prospered in the native soil and climate; if their fancies took them to exotic jacarandas and Himalayan orchids, so be it. The scene would change slowly during the day to represent the transition from rosy-fingered dawn to eventide's velvet cloak; and even more slowly to convey the cycle of the seasons. And if the householder felt the need for a little excitement he could conjure up a thunderstorm or blanket of snow.

Mark was the smallest of the EGCol directors but he was the most ebullient. As he made his presentation to the Board his eyes sparkled, his lips salivated and his short bristly hair crackled with static electricity The others reacted according to their natures: Keith Kendall maintained an air of impassivity as befits one who has to evaluate the commercial worth of a project unaffected by personal inclinations; James Percival, freckled and ginger-haired, nodded in assent from time to time as he saw opportunities for his manufacturing capacity; Lance Mere, tall and handsome, permitted himself an encouraging smile as the market potential of the proposal unfolded in his mind; and Hector, thin and twisted, racked backwards and forwards in his enormous chair at the head of the great oval table, muttering to himself.

Mark paused in his presentation, smiled and said:

"That brings me to the point where we - or, rather, our predecessors - had reached two years ago. We now have the option of starting where we left off without any further development and making (I believe Mr Kendall will bear me out on this) a substantial return on our capital. But, I suggest, we also have the option of extending the already valuable use of this technology to more advanced applications. For example, by exploiting the techniques of virtual reality realisation, our clients will not only be able to construct and delight in their own gardens, they will - while still in the comfort of their arm-chairs - be able to wander about, perhaps rest for a while in the summer-house or gaze at the wild-life in the pond. (Perhaps we can borrow some of your tadpoles when we're shooting that part, Keith). [Laughter].

"But why confine ourselves to gardens? Once the video projectors and screens are in place, our clients will be able to travel vicariously anywhere in the world and experience virtually anything that can be experienced. Who wouldn't jump at the chance of absorbing the glory that was Greece without having to endure the dreadful Greek food and drink or wrestling with the dreadful Greek language? Why not lie amongst the bronzed bodies on Bondi Beach then swim in the waters of the coral reef? Why not drive a buggy on the moon? The possibilities are boundless!"

The Board congratulated Mark on his presentation and duly authorised implementation of the more advanced form of the project.

This was one of the occasions when Hector, more out of politeness than interest, asked whether I had anything to contribute before he closed the session.

"Thank you, chairman," I said. "I am glad to have this opportunity to bring a modest proposal to the attention of the Board. First, I must say how gratifying it is to see how successful the company has become under its new leadership. Admittedly, it is too early to expect to see positive cash flows from the projects you have launched, but the fact that they have all been unreservedly endorsed by your banks indicates that the financial institutions are convinced you are a rising star At the same time you have not moved one iota from the high ethical principles which are the foundation stones of the company ethos."

Hector thoroughly enjoyed this flattery but didn't like to display his pleasure. "Get on with it!" he snapped, wriggling in his chair.

"I suggest that now is the time," I went on, "to demonstrate that the company will play a positive role in local community activities. You may recall from your knowledge of local history that nearly a century ago Boskey Common and Boskey Village together acquired an international reputation as a centre for artistic activities. This reputation has, alas, long since been extinguished. But imagine the good publicity that would accrue to Boskey in general and EGCol in particular if your company were to sponsor an artistic revival - perhaps, just a month-long festival at first, then gradually working up to an unbroken cycle of artistic creation."

"I trust you remember, Melvyn," interrupted Hector, "that when I presented my business philosophy to the crowds in Charlies Fields all those months ago, I specifically undertook not to fawn to the government or the media by undertaking specious public relations exercises."

"I do indeed, Chairman," I said, "and I wholeheartedly support that stance. But what I am suggesting is a drive to revive a local spirit that has long been expiring but which, I am sure, could be made vibrant again. If, at the same time, EGCol happens to attract some positive publicity, then that's a bonus!"

Hector swivelled his chair to gaze round the table. "Well?" he asked "What does the Board think of Melvyn's proposal?"

Keith Kendall was the first to reply.

"We mustn't delude ourselves," he said, "that we can undertake such a mission without expenditure of money and effort. However delightful this might be to the community and whatever good impressions of the company this effort might create, I have to say there is no way I can put a figure on the financial benefit of goodwill."

"Thank you," said Hector. "I wouldn't have expected you to respond in any other way. What about you, James?"

"I like the idea," said James Percival. "It would attract a lot of creative types to live in the neighbourhood. They're just the sort of people we will need as a source of recruitment as the company expands."

Mark agreed; he thought it was a splendid idea.

Finally, Hector turned to his Managing Director. "Lance?"

Lance was cautious. "I must confess," he said, "that I am not a very artistic person. I can't tell Bach from Bartok and the only play I like is a good game of rugger. Having said that, I do understand that many people do enjoy such pastimes and I am able to appreciate that our sponsoring them would bring us credit. So I don't want to say anything against the proposal in principle.

"However, a word of warning. I know from my experience with my previous employers that these fringe activities have to be extremely well performed and organised if they are to be done at all; it will certainly not redound to the credit of the company if they are staged by incompetent amateurs. And we would be fooling ourselves if we believed that we around this table together with our in-line staff can organise a festival in our spare time. We will need an experienced - is the right term 'impressario'? - on a full-time basis. If such a person is appointed I would be happy to back them with all the management and organisational skills at my disposal."

"Thank you, gentlemen," said Hector. "I gather that Melvyn's proposal has your support. However, I do acknowledge the force behind Lance's contribution, namely, that we will need a highly experienced and talented person to take control of our artistic activities. I will get our head-hunters to initiate a search right away."

And that is how EGCol and Boskey came to be the artistic centre of Hertfordshire, indeed, of the whole of the southern half of Britain. When it became apparent to the world at large that Boskey had, once again, achieved an international reputation for the arts, Hector and Gwendoline Pennington were happy to accept the credit for its creation; I suppose that's only fair - they would have to have taken the blame had things gone wrong. So I have never grumbled about the lack of recognition about my formative role; I just went back to my humble dwelling and dreamed up a few more far-reaching ideas.

Hector found his arts administrator in the person of Gavin Wain. Gavin had been Director of Corporate Relations with one of the water companies; he was also a director of the East Midlands Opera Company and a judge in the annual Sugar awards for three-dimensional videos. He was a small bald leprechaun-like Irishman, dapper in dress and jovial in manner. Within his first week with the company he had established friendly relations with everyone in the EGCol office; he took particular care to nurture a warm liaison with Lance Mere, who he correctly identified as the king-pin of the organisation. He formed another ally in Gwendoline, who found the world of art and artists far more glamorous than EGCol's normal activities. She expressed great interest in drama, hinting that she was no mean actress herself and urged that the creation of a theatre and a drama group should be high amongst Gavin's priorities.

Gavin found the basis of his theatre in the shell of what had once been the huge Gothic house of Otto von Bonnberger, a Victorian painter who had dominated the Boskey scene in the earlier decades of the twentieth century. The upper part of the house had virtually been destroyed by fire but the great ground floor ballroom was largely intact. Soon, with the aid of James Percival's designs and Lance Mere's management skills, a theatre emerged replete with every modern device in lighting, robotic scene-shifting, electronic sound generation and ambient atmospheric control.

Gavin also set about acquiring some of the quaint old 1930s 'suntrap' villas that still remained in the side streets off the main road to Colneford and converting them into studios for painters, potters, composers and mixed-media craftpersons. It was a colourful sight when these creatures emerged at night from their villas, dressed in caftans, denims and laced-up boots (infallible indications of an artistic temperament) to congregate in the long disused circular turning spaces for cars at the end of cul-de-sacs; there they would light fires and sing plaintive songs about destitution in Liverpool in dear days beyond recall.

The dawning of EGCol's artistic era was celebrated by a special gala evening in Gavin's new theatre. Entrance was free and EGCol's employees had been encouraged to mount the stage and display their talents. There were singers, dancers and players of keyboard laser colour generators; I even did a little turn myself - nothing exceptional, just some totally baffling magic - but I was outshone by a young man who juggled four laptop computers ultrasonically linked to visual displays, rapidly manipulating the keys each time one of them fell into his hands so that there seemed to be above his head an unbroken arc of continually changing geometric patterns.

At the end of it all, Hector led Gwendoline on to the stage in front of a cheering audience. He gave a short speech about EGCol's support for the arts, of how this evening was but a modest beginning of great things that were to come and that he was delighted to name this the 'Gwendoline Theatre'. He then thanked all who had taken part and especially Gavin Wain and Lance Mere for their splendid efforts. These two worthies were sitting in the front row and blushed becomingly. At this point Gwendoline directed, from the stage, a long fluttering wink at Lance which was seen by everyone in the theatre except her husband.

Just before the Penningtons were about to depart for their home, Hector was called to the Communications Room where a message awaited him. It was that Elaine had given birth to a baby boy.

Hector's mind flashed back to the sofa in his office and Elaine's flailing ribbons and her cries of surprise rather than of passion or pain. He had a sudden burst of exultation - he had a son! Then - despair, disgust. This son could never succeed him as Chairman of EGCol and Gwendoline must never know of his existence. The boy was to be called Mortimer.

CHAPTER SEVEN

Hector sat at the end of the great oval table and beamed with satisfaction. Lance Mere had reported that the Dried Tadpole project was proceeding well: the giant meshes and the microwave oven towers were working to specification with only the most trivial of hitches (occasionally - very occasionally - batches of tadpoles had been emerging a trifle on the rare side); the number of farming tanks had been increased to meet accelerating demand; and there was every chance that the financial break-even point would be reached in less than four years instead of the budgeted five.

A new business plan had been presented that afternoon and had been accepted by the Board. The idea had originated from Mark, the Marketing Director, and had been subjected to Keith Kendall's usual thorough financial analysis. Mark had pointed out that although transport to the supermarket and other shops was now relatively easy, thanks to the public cable-car system, many shoppers - particularly the elderly and otherwise disadvantaged - who hadn't cars of their own, were fatigued by lugging great trolleys of goods from one store to another and to and fro the cable-car terminus. Moreover the traditional wire trolleys were far too small for the customary one month's supplies. If, however, purchases could be lifted a couple of metres above the ground by helium-filled balloons, shoppers would be relieved of their burdens. The balloons, towed along by cords, would be zeppelin-shaped to ease directional control and might have rudders activated by wires connected to the shoppers' gloves; and, to avoid entanglement, they would be electrically charged to the same polarity as one another and so be mutually repulsive. Their cost would be offset by seeking revenue from advertising slogans borne on their flanks; grander versions, belonging to the nobility, would eschew such vulgarity and would display the family hatchments instead.

The proposal had all the characteristics of a true EGCol project: helium was inherently safe; the balloons would be of most benefit to the poor and handicapped; and if they were to be brightly-coloured and sport amusing slogans, they would bring glamour and entertainment to the shopping scene. There was an export potential, too: the balloons could literally lift the burdens from the shoulders of those millions of people in the Third World whose lot in life it was to be little more than pack animals; come to that, the pack animals would benefit as well. Both the Ministry of Overseas Aid & Export and The Save The Dobbin Fund could be relied upon to support the proposal.

The anniversary of Hector's assumption of the chairmanship was approaching. He decided to stage a party both to celebrate a year of successful trading and to launch the exciting new balloon project. He envisaged having marquees and trestle-tables in the ground of Dromdeal Tower where there would be all kinds of drinks, snacks, sweetmeats, cakes and great gobbets of mock meat turning on the open-air spit. Jugglers and troubadours would wander through the crowds; and EGCol employees and their spouses would be encouraged to join in the rustic pastimes of country dancing, tug o' war contests, pig-wrestling and emasculating the sheep. Gwendoline was pleased with the idea and enthusiastically set about organising the show.

The great day dawned and was quite delightful. Everyone in EGCol, from the directors down to the catering staff, were there in their jolliest clothes, ambling over the sunlit lawns, exploring paths through the shrubbery and picking their way through the formal mazes. Hector moved amongst them deliberately seeking out every member of his staff, shaking their hands, thanking for their efforts over the past year and promising them a rise or a bonus.

There was one individual, however, whose hand was never shaken, who was never thanked for past efforts and who wasn't promised a rise in salary. This was Laurence Fuller, a senior software engineer. At first he thought this neglect was an oversight and that he would be thanked and rewarded like the others. But as the day went on he began to realise that he was being consciously avoided; every time he and Hector found themselves on the same path or the same patch of lawn, Hector would look embarrassed and scuttle sideways like a startled crab. I asked one or two of his colleagues why Laurence was being cold-shouldered in this way. They said that although he had many positive attributes (he was good-looking and well-built; he was good at his job, indeed, none better; and he had worked loyally in EGCol's cause during the year) he unfortunately lacked the flamboyance, the dash and the drive that Hector so much admired. I could see their point: even on this day of enjoyment and merry-making, Laurence was wearing dark patched clothes, scuffed boots and a hang-dog expression. (I later learned that he was impoverished by having to support a sick mother and sister; but since he had not revealed this worthy but boring fact to EGCol's personnel department he had no-one but himself to complain).

Laurence found the mock-rustic charades becoming increasingly distasteful so he wandered out of the garden and on to the fringe of Edgemore Heath. He sat on a wooden bench, rested his head in his hands and stared gloomily across the sward. After a while he became aware that two young ladies were walking across the cricket pitch towards him. One was blonde, the other brunette; both were plump and pretty, if a trifle tarty.

"Hallo, Laurence," said the blonde. "I'm Doreen."

"Hallo, Laurence," said the brunette. "I'm Noreen."

"Good afternoon, ladies," responded Laurence politely "How did you know my name?"

"There's a lot we know about you," said Doreen. "Isn't there, Noreen?"

"There certainly is, Doreen," said Noreen. "The things we know about you!"

"What things?" asked Laurence, alarmed.

"Never mind about that!" said Doreen briskly. "We can't stand here all day gossiping. We've been sent to fetch you by our mistress and unless we're back in double-quick time we'll be in deep trouble."

"Hairbrush on bottom time!" elaborated Noreen.

"Who is your mistress?" asked Laurence, rapidly finding the

conversation becoming too slippery to grasp.

"You'll soon see," said Doreen. "You'll be gob-smacked when you find out! Won't he, Noreen?"

"I'll go further," said Noreen. "He'll be banjaxed! Come on, follow us."

The girls turned away from Laurence, linked arms across shoulders and started to walk back across the cricket field. After a moment's hesitation, Laurence rose from the bench and followed them. When they reached the edge of the field the girls turned down a narrow path through the trees, chattering and laughing together like a pair of cockatoos. Laurence continued to follow them, greatly wondering. The woods became more and more dense and darkling until, suddenly, the path opened out into a clearing and there was the most elegant marquee Laurence had ever beheld. It was decorated in broad royal blue and silver stripes with golden fleurs-de-lys dotted in the blue; at each corner of the roofing little golden lions gaped in mock menace over quartered shields. A faint sound of harpsichords floated from therein. Doreen and Noreen drew aside the laps of the silken door and indicated Laurence to enter.

Laurence hesitantly stepped through the entrance then reeled back from the heady atmosphere of incense, darkness and Scarlatti. He could just make out exquisite pieces of Regency furniture around the edge of the marquee and crystal-topped tables bearing fluted goblets and bowls of potpourri. At the centre of this intoxicating tableau there was a large chaise-longue striped in the same blue and silver of the tenting; and on the chaise-longue there stretched a langorous lady. Laurence sidled up diffidently and bent over the gracefully recumbent form... and then started back with a yelp of surprise. Because lying there, in that tent on Edgemore Heath, was The Most Famous Film Star in the World. She was no longer young: fine lines radiated from her eyes and ligatures tautened in her throat, but she was still astoundingly beautiful. She smiled at Laurence's discomforture and beckoned him close again. He leaned his face towards her.

"There's no need for formal introductions," she murmured. "You're Laurence Fuller, one of EGCol's heroes."

Laurence was choked with astonishment; then he cleared his throat.

"The whole world knows who you are, my lady," he gasped. "You're..."

A hand flicked out and sealed his lips.

"Don't ever mention my name!" she said sharply. "You must never, never, say who I am."

"Very well, said Laurence. "But how did you know...?"

"Who you are?" laughed the lady. "I and my two young handmaidens have been following you for weeks. But first, I must tell you a little about myself. In my professional life I have played every major female role from Clytemnestra to the Princess of Wales - and some male parts as well. I have received every award from best supporting actress to lifetime achievement. There is nothing more I wish to act, direct or even see. During all those years of playing the great lover I have never had the time or opportunity for being loved myself. So I have abandoned taking the role of lover and I'm now devoting myself to the real thing. I wander the world with my two maids (some rudely call them my procuresses) and - you might find this distasteful - ensnare virile young men. Doreen saw you by accident two weeks ago and brought me in disguise to spy on you. I knew immediately you must be my next great love. We were sure you would wander into our net sooner or later."

"But, of all the millions of men in the world," asked Laurence. "Why choose me?"

"Who can tell? Who can tell?" murmured the lady reflectively. "It's an eternal mystery. I suppose in your case it was a combination of good looks, superb physique and little-boy-lost look. In a world of braggarts, you have genuine humility and modesty. You must have attracted the lover and the mother in me simultaneously. Tell me, could you learn to love me?"

"I can't imagine anything easier... or more wonderful."

"Good! For, from now on, you're going to possess me body and soul - something which millions of men have been longing to do for thirty years. Not only that, I will see to it that your miserable rags are replaced by the most stylish clothes and that you will have all the money you need and plenty to spare."

"For God's sale!" shouted Laurence. "I don't want payment!"

"This isn't payment, my sweet," laughed the lady. "It's just that when you become the consort of the most celebrated woman in the world, you must be properly accoutred - even though we meet only in secret."

"In secret?"

"Yes, that must be an essential part of our arrangement. We will meet as often as we can - and particularly when you call for me - but it must always be in secret. We must never be seen together. You must understand I must still preserve my aura of mysterious unapproachability You must never mention, even to your mother or your sister, that there is any relationship between us or, indeed, that you have ever met me."

"That should be easy," said Laurence. "No-one would ever believe me if I did!"

Laurence returned to his little home in The Furrows in the early hours of the next morning. His mother and sister were astonished at the change in his appearance: it was as though a lantern had been lit in a long-defunct lighthouse. They were even more astonished when messengers arrived throughout the day bringing in armfuls of the smartest clothes. He was hard put to explain his good fortune.

His change in appearance and demeanour was immediately noted when he returned to the EGCol offices the following week; Hector admonished himself for treating such a valuable and personable young manager so shabbily. Laurence's new fortune seemed boundless: fresh clothes, jewels and masculine toilet preparations appeared almost every week; his bank balance was regularly enhanced from a mysterious source; and, best of all by far, were the frequent visits by night by The Most Famous Film Star in the World and the hours of sensual delight they spent together.

One day, Gwendoline and two of her friends came to the EGCol office to have lunch with Hector. When they had finished their meal Gwendoline looked out of the window and saw Laurence, Mark and Keith Kendall strolling through the office gardens. She called Hector's secretary over to the window.

"I know those two gentlemen," she said, pointing down to Mark and Keith, "but I don't think I have seen the other one before."

"That's Laurence Fuller," said the secretary. "Actually, he's been with us for quite a long time but he seems to have become more noticeable recently."

"Girls," said Gwendoline to her friends, "tittivate yourselves. We're going to bring colour and glamour into the lives of those poor workers."

The three young ladies went down to the ground floor and wandered, seemingly aimlessly through the gardens. Soon, with little cries of delighted surprise, they encountered the three heroes. By a series of winks and nudges, Gwendoline paired off her friends with Mark and Keith and was thus able to cut Laurence off from the group and shepherd him step by step into the shrubbery.

"I don't think we have met, have we?" she asked, turning sideways to give Laurence an unhindered view of her full-length profile.

"I'm Laurence Fuller," he said shyly. "I'm in the software engineering department."

"That must be fascinating. And do you know who I am?"

"Oh, yes, of course. You're the Chairman's wife, Mrs Pennington."

"There's no need for the 'Mrs Pennington'. I'm Gwendoline."

"Yes... er... Gwendoline."

"I have a confession. I haven't lured you away from the others just for mutual introductions. I have an ulterior motive. Tell me, Laurence, have you ever thought of appearing in the Boskey Dramatic Society productions? With your good looks and bearing you could be just the young male lead we have been waiting for. If you know anything about me at all, you'll know I'm an enthusiastic supporter of the Arts and I'm always on the lookout for fresh talent."

"Oh, no, really, Mrs Penn... Gwendoline, that's not my scene at all. I'm terribly bad in public. I would dry up on the stage. I'm an awful actor."

"Oh, come now, no false modesty. With a little coaching you would be first rate - I can see it in you. In fact, I would be happy to teach you myself."

"That's very good of you, but really, it's not for me. I would be a disaster."

"Nonsense! You know, it's a splendid stroke of good fortune that I came across you today. The Society's next production will be a play based on the lives of Heloise and Abelard. As it happens I will be playing Heloise but we haven't cast anyone yet for Abelard. You would be ideal for the part."

"I couldn't possibly..."

"Let's see if I can tempt you. There's a marvellous scene when the two lovers are naked together in bed. We would have to be discreet during public performances, of course, but think of the fun we could have rehearsing!"

Laurence was becoming hot and bothered. Such an unabashed assault by the boss's wife was not a situation he had had to cope with in previous employment. He responded with shocked acerbity.

"I must repeat, Mrs Pennington, this is not for me!"

Gwendoline was, by now, deeply offended by this series of rebuffs from a company employee. She changed her tone from coaxing to cutting.

"What's the matter with you? Are you gay?"

"Certainly not!"

"Then what? Are you committed to someone else?"

Laurence hung his head in anguish and nodded dumbly.

"Oh, so I have a rival, do I? But don't you know, hasn't anyone told you, can't you see with your own eyes, that I am exceptionally beautiful?"

Laurence looked up and dropped his eyes again.

"Why don't you answer?" demanded Gwendoline. "Am I not more beautiful than this woman of yours?"

Laurence was stung beyond caution. He raised his head and looked her straight in the eyes.

"Mrs Pennington," he said, "the lady I'm committed to is far, far more beautiful than you."

(Perhaps it was his imagination, but even as he spoke these words he heard a distant cry of despair).

Gwendoline gave a little scream of fury and ran off to find her friends. They were soon receiving a highly-coloured version of her encounter with Laurence in which, apparently, he had gratuitously insulted her by implying she was ugly. They urged the weeping wretch to return to the office and report the affair to Hector. Hector was properly enraged; he did not know, of course - and Laurence did not enlighten him - that Gwendoline had attempted to seduce his employee. All he could gather was this man had unfavourably compared Gwendoline - universally regarded as a beauty non-pareil - with some unknown floozy of his own. Laurence was instructed to leave the office immediately and await judgement.

That night Laurence called desperately to his lady to visit him, but she didn't come. He knew why, of course: he had broken the terms of their agreement. Mark and Keith Kendall called on him next morning with an ultimatum from Hector: Laurence was to apologise to Gwendoline and Hector in public, repudiating the ridiculous notion that there was anybody more beautiful than the Chairman's wife; otherwise he would be dismissed from the company and would not be offered employment elsewhere in Boskey again. Laurence refused to apologise.

"I cannot lie," he said. "My lady is far, far, more beautiful than Gwendoline."

His friends shook their heads sadly and returned to Hector with his reply. All that night Laurence called out desperately for his lady, but she didn't come. He knew he had no-one but himself to blame.

The next morning Mark and Keith visited him again. Hector had acknowledged that Laurence was good at his work and that he had possibly been unjustly treated on the day of the garden party. He would be given a second chance to apologise. Laurence refused again.

"No," he repeated, "my lady is far, far, more beautiful than Gwendoline."

Mark and Keith went away, more despondent than ever about their colleague's pigheadedness.

Later that morning the receptionist at the EGCol office building was startled to find two pretty plump girls standing before her.

"We're Doreen and Noreen," they said in chorus. "Could you please tell your Chairman we have a message for him?"

Hector was so intrigued by the receptionist's account that he hurried down to the reception area.

"I hope you're not wasting my time," he said gruffly.

"We're emiss... emiss..." stuttered Doreen.

"... aries," completed Noreen, "to deliver an important message."

"You have been very harsh on Laurence, you know," said Doreen. "He hasn't behaved badly at all."

"That's right!" cried Noreen. "He was provoked beyond all reason!"

"Wait here," said Hector. "I'll send someone to fetch him."

Within fifteen minutes Laurence had been escorted from his home and was standing with Hector and the two girls and a little knot of bystanders who were slowly gathering.

"Fuller," said Hector sternly, "I want you to look at these two young ladies and tell me if either of them was the one you said was more beautiful than my wife."

Laurence eyed them briefly as they collapsed, giggling, into each other's arms.

"Good lord, no, sir!" he said. "Neither of them is my lady."

Doreen and Noreen regained their composure.

"We have a message from our mistress," said Doreen, "and I do advise you to do as she says."

"She says," continued Noreen, "that you, Mr Pennington, and your wife, Gwendoline, and anybody else concerned in this matter should be in Charlie's Fields at ten o'clock tomorrow morning."

They turned, arms about shoulders, and twittered back towards the Heath.

Laurence was sent home under escort. He didn't attempt to call upon his lady that night. He sat with his head in his hands in tearful silence.

Mark and Keith went to Laurence's house for the third time the next morning and accompanied him to Charlie's Fields. At ten o'clock a sizable crowd had gathered, including Hector and Gwendoline on their private bench. Hector could see no logical reason why he should interrupt his busy schedule to behave as the girls had requested; but he was intrigued and felt impelled to follow this little adventure through to its end. For her part, Gwendoline had gained the impression that the event in Charlie's Fields was to be some sort of trial of Laurence's behaviour and gleefully anticipated a Guilty verdict and his public humiliation. So they had agreed, for their various reasons, that they should be present that morning and let it be known to their friends and colleagues that some sort of curious episode was to be expected.

The buzz of the crowd's conversation was suddenly hushed. A faint humming sound could be heard floating through the air; a few seconds later a biplane could be discerned skimming through the trees. It was that most elegant of aircraft, a de Havilland Dragon Rapide. It circled three times overhead and then swooped in for a perfect landing on the cricket pitch. Now all could see that its fuselage was royal blue, its wings were silver and there were fleurs-de-lys patterning the blue.

When the plane had come to rest, a door opened, a short ladder was dropped to the ground and out stepped The Most Famous Film Star in the World. She had a profile like Nefertiti's, her hair flowed down in luxuriant gold and silver waves, her neck was a perfect arabesque, her figure was as full and as proud as a Greek goddess's and her legs were as long and as elegant as a giraffe's. A cry of excited admiration came from the crown as she walked across the field to where the EGCol group was seated.

"Indeed!" murmured a hundred voices. "She is more beautiful, far, far, more beautiful than Gwendoline!"

The lady came up to Laurence and took him by the hand. Without a word they walked back across the field to where the plane was waiting. They climbed in, the door closed, the plane taxied away gathering speed, then took off and circled three times over the field before disappearing into the distance.

And they were never seen again.

CHAPTER EIGHT

Several people had suggested to Hector, as he approached the fifth anniversary of his assumption of EGCol's chairmanship, that this might be the occasion for a special celebration. But he was unenthusiastic. He would refer curtly to the increasing variety and fame of his arts centre and then testily observe that any further celebration would be superfluous; it would detract attention from the many worthy activities already under way and, moreover, would add to his non-core business costs. The fact was, as I could detect from my personal and electronic observations, that Hector was in a black mood. His personal contributions to the work of his company were as brilliant as ever but he was beginning to realise that he was still immature and ill-equipped to deal with problems of a non-intellectual nature. For instance, his analytical review of the timings of each stage of the Grilled Tadpole operation had led to an improvement of over 9% in throughput; but when the nature of the project was hysterically denigrated by The Friends of Jeremy Fisher (a society of elderly lady frog-fanciers), his attempts to cool their wrath was dreadfully inept - indeed, he upset them so much that several of his installations were vandalised by their shrill commando squads.

I happened to be present at the regular Board meeting on that very anniversary Hector made no attempt to hide his irritability; he twisted about in his chair and shuffled and re-shuffled his papers. The Board members, sitting around the great oval table, fidgeted in sympathy with their Chairman's moods; all, that is, except Lance Mere, who remained erect and still, seemingly impervious to the thunderous atmosphere. Fortunately most of the meeting was made up of routine progress reports with little new business to consider so no potential new projects were blighted at birth by being assessed by troubled minds.

The last item on the agenda was to be a plea by middle-management grades to have more time off for study in the conference room when it was not otherwise in use. Board papers had been circulated in advance and the verbal presentation was to be made by Ursula Blanchard, the staff representative of the appropriate grades. She was politely invited into the Board room by Keith Kendall and told somewhat curtly by Hector to sit down and say her piece. She was dressed in a white linen sheath with circlets of black and gold ribbons descending from her shoulders and hips; at her throat she wore a mock-Celtic brooch depicting a jewelled sword piercing a circular shield. The Board members had all read her paper the previous evening and had already made up their minds about her proposals. It had been a long and boring day and they were somnolent, so our attention on what she was actually saying was ill-focussed until we heard Hector snapping "Wait a bit, Blanchard, what you are saying bears no relationship to the title of the agenda item nor the subject-matter of your paper."

"Quite right, Chairman, it doesn't," replied Ursula coolly. "It's much more important. We underlings rarely have the chance to address the Board and I couldn't let this opportunity slip by. You can have me thrown out if you like, but I trust you will be civil enough to listen to what I have to say."

Hector glanced round the table. Most of us had woken up by now and were becoming interested in this sparky young woman. Hector would have preferred to have terminated the discussion there and then, but, seeing she had grasped our attention, he turned back to her and said "Very well, get on."

"Thank you, chairman," she said. "Perhaps I had better start again.

"Gentlemen, I and many of my colleagues are proud to be working for a company that has 'In Deed to Goodness' as its slogan. I think we would all agree that the latter decades of the last century were characterised by a single-minded pursuit of profit, the retreat of all social planning in the face of 'market forces' and a complacent acceptance that companies and individuals could go to the wall if they didn't meet the criteria of financial success. Eventually the British people came to regard these principles with distaste and rejected them. I expect you, Chairman, are proud that the past generations of Penningtons who created this company were part of the great movement against the materialistic society and I expect you would maintain that the company today is maintaining that great tradition.

"But is it? I note that all the projects currently under way have been scrutinised not only as to whether they meet your ethical objectives but also whether they are likely to achieve long-term profitable growth. Nothing wrong with that, you might say -after all, no profit: no project; no project: no means of upholding your ethical principles. You may also claim that a significant proportion of the profits you do make is siphoned off into your artistic community activities. All very worthy. But am I not correct in observing that these artistic side-shoots have become a tourist attraction and have generated a flourishing secondary trade; and so, in turn, have added further to the profits of the company? And are not the profits of your company now so high that you can not only pay substantial dividends to your shareholders, you can also vote enormous increases in your own emoluments. In short, are not the ethical considerations taking second place?"

Hector scowled from the recesses of his chair. "What are you suggesting?" he asked. "That we should direct ourselves to making losses?"

"Please don't patronise me," replied the young woman. "I'm not totally daft. What I am suggesting is..."

At this point something about her disturbed me. I had certainly seen her in the office and I knew she really was the staff representative. But was there not some other context in which she had impinged upon my memory? I made my excuses to Hector, hurriedly left the Board Room and scuttled along to my little den. Once there, I switched on my monitor so I could still hear Ursula Blanchard's speech to the Board.

"... if you are not only to continue, but to build upon and extend the work of your father and grandfather, you must aspire to a really great achievement. I think I speak for all the staff when I say that we would welcome being members of an organisation that was celebrated throughout the world for doing something really noble - provided, of course, our remuneration and working conditions were satisfactory."

I was riffling through the staff records on my screen. At last - here we were - Ursula Blanchard, age 26, been with the company for three years, socio-economic group 2B, racial group 1C...

"And what, dear lady," sneered Hector, "would this 'noble achievement' consist of?"

"No less," she replied boldly, "than to bring Goodness and Peace to the world. I don't know - I'm sure your collective brains are better than mine - whether you can actually foster Goodness or whether you achieve the same result by driving out evil. I don't suppose it matters whether you follow the positive or negative paths if the final result is the same."

I switched my screen to the Board Room and could see the directors boggling with astonishment. Hector creased into a sardonic smile and spoke:

"And if we found the formula to this remarkable end, by what means should we put it into effect?"

"Perhaps you can find the right chemical or drug or whatever it is," responded Ursula smoothly "and drop it into the drinking water... just as they did with fluoride fifty years ago. That did no end of good to the nation's teeth - I want you to do the same to the nation's morals."

Half my attention was with Ursula's words and the other half with her records. I rapidly zipped through her educational and training achievements, her debts and other financial obligations, her sexual orientation and attachments, memberships of parties, societies and recreational groups, and then... ah! this is what I was looking for... whilst working in one of EGCol's provincial offices, she had had an affair with a young man who was rejected by her family; there had been a fight between the young man and her brother in which her brother had been killed. And this young man of hers, her brother's killer, was... Lance Mere's brother! Clearly she had inveigled her way into the

Board meeting under the guise of making a presentation in order to exact revenge!

I rushed back to the Board room. Ursula Blanchard had finished her speech and was inviting questions from the directors. Just as I was about to sit down, she said:

"It's terribly hot in here, gentlemen. May I remove my upper circlet?"

"Feel free," snapped Hector.

She moved to undo the sword-and-shield clasp at her throat. As soon as it was free I threw myself at her and snatched it from her hands; I pulled at the handle of the little sword and out slid a hyperdemic syringe. I plunged it straight into the girl's arm and she fell back into her chair with scarcely a sigh.

"Melvyn!" shouted Hector "What have you done? What is the meaning of this?"

"This girl's brother," I explained, "was recently killed in a fight with none other than Lance Mere's brother". [Mere leapt to his feet in astonishment]. "The only motive for her presentation to you this afternoon was so that she could remove her brooch and stab the Managing Director He would have died in ten minutes."

"Does this mean you have just killed her?" shouted Hector.

"Not if we can get her to my room quickly," I said. "I have a concoction of mugwort, tutsan, feverfew and dittany of Crete which should be an effective antidote". (I had none of these ghastly herbs really, but I liked to convey the impression I had powers of a warlock. In fact, she had used a fairly conventional poison, the counter to which was readily available).

Hector called the meeting to order; as you might imagine, the Board was somewhat unsettled.

"What this afternoon's events have brought home to us," said Hector, "is the need to review our personal protection against assault. I am not referring to the company's general security measures - if we introduced any more checks and passwords we would arouse the hostility and derision of the staff. I am talking about our own individual safety from the sort of attack that was thwarted just in time this afternoon. I am not going to lay down any standard methods; it would be best if we each devised our own. Meanwhile, I declare this meeting is in abeyance; it will be resumed in a few days time."

I hurried back to my room where Ursula was supine on my couch. After one injection she was sitting up and rubbing her eyes.

"Oh, it's you," she said. "I might have guessed you were on to me when you rushed out of the Board Room. But what do you intend to do? After all, I haven't assaulted anyone - it was you who assaulted me!"

"What you need, my girl," I said sternly, "is a jolly good spanking."

"Oh, you're one of those, are you?" she grinned coquettishly. I was shocked: "No, I am certainly not one of those!" I spluttered. "I'm going to send you back up North where you came from."

And she went. But, sometimes, late at night, when I catch a glimpse of my hairbrush on my dressing table...

I monitored Hector closely during the next few days. He had been badly shaken by the incident but he said nothing about it to Gwendoline; instead, telling his wife he had late business at the office, he visited his mother and sought her advice. Lady Iris gravely considered the problem and said:

"There's no sort of armour that can protect you against really determined assault or assassination. The best you can do is to have immediate access to some means of recovery from bodily harm. (I mean against the effects of drugs, poisons or wounds; no one can do much for you if you're decapitated; microsurgeons haven't yet perfected the technique for head replacement - there hasn't been much demand). The most accomplished person I know in the field of recuperative medicine is Elaine. You should go and see her."

Lady Iris was surprised to see Hector's face suffuse with a roseate flush; she was unaware of his past liaison with her half-sister.

"I don't know where she lives." stuttered Hector. "I've only met her at marriages and funerals and the occasional visit to the office."

"Then you have an experience in store," said his mother. "She lives at the far side of the lake in Edgemore Woods. Take your cable car to Edgemore Heath, walk to the edge of the lake and you will find a little dinghy tethered to a tree. Row across the lake to the Flemish-looking house at the far side of the lake and there you will find Elaine. It will probably be the only physical exercise you have taken in years."

"What about her husband and daughter?" asked Hector nervously. "Will they be at home?"

"Her husband left her about five years ago and took their daughter with him. I understand there had been a serious marital disturbance, but I never went into the details."

Hector muttered his thanks and left but it took him another three days to build up enough bravado to visit his quandam inamorata. As his mother had foretold, he found a small boat awaiting him at the lakeside; he rowed clumsily and painfully across the lake to the Dutch-gabled dark brick house. Elaine was pleased to see him.

"I knew you would come," she said, "but I wasn't sure when. We have some important matters to discuss."

"Oh, you know already, do you?" said Hector. "You have started thinking about it?"

"Of course I've been thinking about it. It affects not only the here-and-now but future generations of Penningtons."

"Quite so. (By the way, do you have anything for blistered hands? That boat of yours...) It was mother who recommended I should see you. She said you were particularly skilled in devising cures and antidotes..."

"Cures and antidotes!" Elaine interrupted. "I though you had come here to talk about our son's future."

"Our son's future! But he isn't five years old yet!"

"That's just the right age to start preparing for the future. Surely he will take over the leadership of the business from you - after all, Gwendoline hasn't given you a son yet. Haven't you considered what education and training you are going to give him to prepare him for the chairmanship?"

"Education and training?" (Hector had never given the matter a thought; indeed, he had scarcely given his son a thought. His mind raced wildly).

"Well, if he's to take over from me he will require profound wisdom, extensive knowledge and extraordinary organising ability. I would therefore like something that combined the wise tranquillity of the Buddhists, the educational principles of the Jesuits and the management skills of MIT."

"I have no idea where I could find such an establishment," said Elaine, "so you had better take the child with you and put the matter in hand yourself. But clearly you didn't come here to talk about anything so trifling as your son's future. So what did you want to see me about?"

Hector recounted the story of the Board Room drama, his realisation of his own vulnerability and his mother's advice. "Oh, I see!" said Elaine sardonically "It's your own precious skin you're worrying about. I thought you were supposed to be the hero of the Home Counties! Well, your mother's right, there's little we can do against a good sword thrust or a hail of bullets. But for everything else - drugs, poisons, most wounds and nervous disorders - I have devised an Intelligent Knowledge Based System which can be run on a conventional lap-top and which will advise you on how to overcome virtually every attack upon your person you are likely to encounter. What's more, you don't need a pharmacopoeia of drugs and injections to compose the antidote - the whole operation is carried out electronically. In essence, the method is similar to acupuncture except you don't need needles and you don't need to know the locations of the sensitive areas of the body's surface".

She went on to explain that it was now known that all the ganglia and synapses of the nervous system have unique addresses; and by setting up these addresses by impulses injected into the nervous system, the correct pattern of currents can be generated which act on the brain and counteract almost all ills, poisons and physical damage. Hector was impressed:

"Marvellous! Did you do all this yourself?"

"Well, I must admit I had some assistance from Fay. She's very good at this sort of thing."

"What sort of thing is that?"

"Peculiar highways and by-ways of technology; software tricks known only to the initiated; untrodden areas of arcane knowledge; esoterica. That sort of thing."

She left the room and returned with a small titanium case; inside there was a lap-top computer and what appeared to be a pair of large ear-phones.

Hector placed the little computer on his lap and tapped in a few symptoms at random; almost instantly the screen displayed the name of a poison and instructed him to apply the pair of foam-covered pads to his temples. He was about to obey when Elaine snatched the pads from his hands.

"Don't be a fool!" she shouted. "Giving yourself the cure when you haven't got the illness is almost as dangerous as having the illness and not the cure!"

Hector trembled, ashamed at his lack of perception; he thought he could just hear a stream of pulses of almost supersonic frequencies emerging from the pads.

Elaine packed the lap-top back in its titanium case and gave it to Hector; she then disappeared into the rear of the house and returned after a fifteen minutes or so with a small boy and a travelling case.

"What's all this?" asked Hector.

"Have you forgotten?" snapped Elaine. "This is your son, Mortimer, and this case contains all the clothes he will need when he's at school. You're going to look after his education, remember?"

"Don't you have any maternal feelings? Don't you want to love and foster him for as long as possible?"

"Frankly, no!"

"Don't you want to be left alone with him for a few more minutes for that last motherly hug?"

"For God's sake stop blethering and go!"

It's true that the little lad didn't seem too upset at parting from his mother, so Hector picked up the travelling case and the computer and led his son down to the lakeside. The boy clambered into the boat without a wave or even a rearward glance.

After a few strokes Hector held up the titanium case and shouted to Elaine. "By the way, what's this thing called?"

"System for Combating Aids, Blemishes, Brainstorms And Related Disorders... SCABBARD."

Halfway across the lake it struck Hector that he had never spoken to his son before.

"Hallo, son," he said. "I'm your daddy."

"I know," replied the lad gravely.

"What should I call you? Mort? Morty?"

"No, Mortimer. And I would prefer to call you 'father' rather than 'daddy'."

"Very well," Hector rowed on without another word, intimidated by the boy's solemn unwinking stare.

When Hector got back to Boskey Common he went straight to his secretary's office in the EGCol building, with his son trotting beside him. "Isolde," he said, "this is my son, Mortimer. I want you to arrange for him to be sent to a residential school, preferably one of those rough outdoor types; it must be a long way away from here and have very short holidays."

Isolde was startled: she was unaware that Hector had a son - Gwendoline had never mentioned him during her visits to the office. "But, Mr Pennington," she protested, "he's only a little boy!"

"I have just learned on good authority," replied Hector, "that this is the very best time to start. Kindly put it in hand right away."

"And in the meantime, Mr Pennington, will he be staying with you in Dromdeal Tower?"

"Certainly not! Fix him up with a childminder somewhere."

And Hector didn't see his son again for fourteen years.

(You may wonder how I know about this lady-in-the-lake episode when my 'security system' didn't extend beyond Boskey Common and I had long since abandoned my moon-bounce radio system. True, my special powers of clairvoyance and forecasting were as lively as ever, but they didn't extend to giving me verbatim records of conversations several kilometres away The truth is more much prosaic: Hector showed me his new SCABBARD and its IKBS software on the very day of his return from Elaine and told me all about his encounter with her and their son).

Two days later Hector reconvened the Board meeting that had been interrupted by Ursula Blanchard's dramatic intervention. The directors were surprised to be called upon again; there didn't seem much more to discuss.

Hector first asked everyone round the great oval table whether they had implemented some means of improving their personal safety. They all nodded but gave no details. Hector said a few words about his universal cure machine; one almost had the impression he had secured the secret of immortality. Then he said:

"Now let's pick up the discussion where we left off about our mission to spread Goodness. You have had plenty of time to think about it. Can I have your ideas?"

They looked at him in goggling amazement.

"But, Chairman," protested Lance Mere, "surely you don't take all that stuff seriously? That was merely a ploy on Blanchard's part to get into this room and attack me!"

"I certainly do take it seriously," replied Hector. "How the matter came to our attention if of minor importance. I now see that this is our company's mission to which everything else must be subservient. From now on I want all directors and their managers to concentrate on finding the basis of morality so that we can spread the Goodness virus throughout the world."

"Chairman," interrupted Mark, "I'm only a simple-minded administrator and I must confess that I don't know what Goodness and Morality are. I can't define them. Do they mean - as Ursula Blanchard suggested - an absence of evil? Is Goodness the same as Peace, freedom from want and fear, the Rights of Man, the Ten Commandments... or what?"

"I don't want any more arguments or delaying tactics," ruled Hector. "You all know perfectly well what Goodness is. As Doctor Johnson said, 'a dog cannot define a bone but he knows one when he sees one'. This is my final word on the subject: your mission is to discover the means whereby EGCol will be able to disseminate Goodness to all mankind."

Gavin Wain pursed his mouth in my ear. "He's flipped!" he whispered. "He's finally flipped!"

CHAPTER NINE

I look back upon those days when Hector and Gwendoline were still in their twenties as the golden age of Boskey Common. The intellectual brilliance of EGCol's staff was universally acknowledged and the public-spirited essence of its enterprises was never in question. Largely as a consequence of the company's sponsorship, the town had become the national centre of the graphic, aural and performing arts; not a month went by without some sort of festival - whether it be of ballets danced by creatures genetically-created for their specific roles or a revival of post-Renaissance music; or a special screening of the last reel of 'The Magnificent Ambersons' (recently discovered among the charred ruins of a motel in Wisconsin); or a symphony of the elements, in which a sequence of thunder, snow, hail, sunshine, spring breezes and rainbows could run the course of the audience's emotions from terror to exultation. And at the centre of it all was Dromdeal Tower, the magnetic pole of the most celebrated artists, musicians, writers and philosophers of the time. It was - in its day - the Florence of the Medici, the Venice of the Doges, the Washington of the Kennedys, the Camelot of legend.

Although Hector delighted in the respect and admiration focussed upon him, he was not entirely happy. For one thing, he had not had a recent opportunity for demonstrating his personal brilliance; and, secondly, his mission to bring Peace and Goodness to the naughty world had made little discernible progress. Gwendoline, on the other hand, suffered from none of these disappointments; as long as there were handsome men, clever men, brave men or funny men around her, her cup of happiness was o'erflowing. Nor did Hector allow his inner worries to disturb his outer mien; he travelled daily from his home to his office, from his office to public festivals, from public festivals to private functions, all with an unwavering expression of contented creativity.

Hector's life was irreversibly changed - although he did not realise it at the time - when Lance Mere, his Managing Director, organised a two-week visit of a northern ballet company to the Gwendoline Theatre. Lance's particular interest in this company was that its principal ballerina, Grace Halliday was his niece. Lance confessed that he didn't know much about ballet, or, indeed, any of the arts, but he could see that the girl was exceptionally gifted and he was keen to provide a showcase for her talents in the south of England. The Borealis Company (for such they were called) eschewed anything vulgar or showy and concentrated on the old Bournonville classics, with an occasional nod towards comparative modernity by staging gala performances of 'Giselle'. These ethereal works were admirable vehicles for Grace Halliday: she was as light as a flickering flame, as airborne as a fluttering feather, as graceful as a willow tree. (In fact, of course, although painfully slim, she was packed with good solid sinew and muscle). Hector was enchanted by her. He went to her every performance and embarrassed her by the magnificence of his bouquets. Lance Mere arranged for them to meet.

Hector went to her dressing-room at the back of the theatre after a performance of 'La Sylphide'. Grace was found seated like something from a Degas painting, dreamily sponging off her make-up. He was astonished to sense his pulse fluttering as she gracefully accepted his confection of camellias.

"You were quite superb!" he gushed.

"Thank you, Mr Pennington, it's kind of you to say so."

"I'm quite sincere. I've never seen such beauty of movement... such purity of expression."

"That's very perceptive of you, sir. I have trained from childhood to believe that inner purity is the essential basis of external beauty."

"Oh, really?" said Hector, a touch disconcerted. "By the way, there's no need to call me 'Mr Pennington' or 'sir'. 'Hector' will do nicely."

"If you'll forgive me, sir, I'd rather not. I would hate to do anything by word or deed that would give the impression of over-familiarity."

This was not how Hector had planned things at all. Although he still thought her stunningly beautiful, he could feel his ardour cooling minute by minute; his appreciation was becoming increasingly aesthetic and less carnal. He backed to the door, gave an awkward little bow and thanked her again for the delight her performance had given him.

"I'll tell the company how much you enjoyed our little programme, Mr Pennington," she responded primly "It was good of you to call."

When Hector met Lance Mere he extolled the virtues of his stalwart lieutenant's niece.

"She is a remarkably good dancer," agreed Lance. "As you know I'm not in the top decile when it comes to artistic appreciation, but even I can see she's something special. And that's not just because I'm her uncle."

"What's more," enthused Hector, "she has a quite remarkable personality She not only personifies purity and goodness on the stage, she actually seems to - well - radiate it in real life. But I expect you know her better than that, eh, Lance? Come clean, tell the truth, is she a little raver at heart?" Lance could see how his boss's mind was working and smilingly shook his head. "Not at all," he said. "What you see is what she is. We all know the popular theory that girls brought up in religious institutions kick over the traces as soon as they can escape. For Grace, it has been quite the reverse: her parents were hard-drinking hell-raising atheists but as soon as she was able to rid herself of their influence she became a model of sobriety and chastity. She's the nearest approach to a saint in a tutu you're likely to find."

"Does she intend to make dancing her life's work?" asked Hector.

"I doubt it. There's a limit to the number of roles in ballet depicting out-and-out purity of character so if she found some other way of spreading sweetness and light, I'm sure she would take it."

Hector wandered off, pondering.

The next Board meeting started calmly enough. There were the usual routine reports about work in progress (on schedule), the company's financial position (healthy), staff recruitment (satisfactory) and sponsorship of the arts (gratifyingly remarked upon by the media). Then came Mark's informal remarks about the ideas currently floating around in his think tank.

"Two or three of my brightest people," he reported, "are turning their attention to food. The trend to 'healthy' eating that started thirty or forty years ago gathered so much momentum that it's now virtually impossible for the ordinary person on the Clapham cable-car to find the 'hearty meals' and the 'junk food' which were so popular a couple of generations ago. We know there are secret societies who meet clandestinely to gorge themselves on fish-and-chips and hamburgers-and-onions, but this is an activity possible only for the rich and eccentric - the basic materials and the skills needed to prepare them are now exceedingly rare. Nonetheless, my researchers are convinced that there is a rapidly-growing interest amongst ordinary folk in the meals of yesteryear. Whether this is merely nostalgia for a life few of them have ever experienced, or whether there is a fundamental desire for what were once regarded as staple diets, it is difficult to say. All I can report at the moment is that there appears to be a substantial market for food which possesses all the health-giving vitamins, fibre and trace elements we enjoy today, whilst having the appearance, bulk and taste of the victuals of the past."

"May I ask, through you, Chairman," interjected Lance Mere, "whether this objective could not be simply achieved by dosing our standard pabulum with the appropriate tastorisers?"

"I'm afraid not," replied Mark. "Our studies have shown that there is a demand not only for the taste but also for the sight, smell and muscular interactivity between teeth and tongue that old-style food possessed."

"Good God!" snapped Hector "We might as well go back to living in caves! But if we accept for the moment that there is a financially attractive market here, what is there of ethical interest?"

"The ethical aspect," said Mark, "is that if the populace starts the day with a hearty early-twentieth-century breakfast, it sets off to work in a happy frame of mind. We're pretty certain that there is a strong positive co-relation between a contented start to the day and a reduction in accidents, inter-personal conflicts and industrial unrest. To coin a phrase: a happy stomach feeds a happy mind!"

"H'mm," grumbled Hector, unconvinced. "I'm not at all sure that happiness is the same as goodness. Nonetheless, since I can appreciate that a lack of contentedness could lead to a lack of goodness, I am prepared to authorise further investigation, provided there's no significant capital outlay at this stage. What do you propose as your next step?"

"The creation - or should I say 're-creation' - in the laboratory of a simple basic dish: namely the appearance, taste and masticity of fried sausage, bacon, egg and bread, but with the digestive qualities of bran, nuts and dried bananas."

"Proceed," instructed Hector "and report back to the Board in three months."

There was a break whilst Isolde served us with chestnut rock cakes and chalybeate water.

Then came the sensation. Hector rapped the great oval table for attention and announced he had a non-agenda item to introduce.

"Keith," he said, "would you please fetch in here the person waiting in the ante-room."

Keith went out as bid and returned with his ascetic features rigid with astonishment. Entering the room behind him was Lance's niece, the ballerina.

"Gentlemen," said Hector, "let me introduce to you the new member of our Board of Directors - Miss Grace Halliday. She will be assuming the newly-created post of Director of Forward Planning. Grace, I am sure your contributions to our Board meetings will be of immense benefit to our company; and I trust your time with us will be a happy and rewarding experience."

Grace sank gracefully into a vacant chair with a murmur of thanks whilst the rest of the Board looked from one to another, agape. Had

Hector lost all reason in bringing this elfin creature into the highest management level of a major company? Was he besotted with the girl? What would the staff think?... there were scores of people with the drive, experience and creativity to justify their having a superior claim to director status. Then, feeling Hector's burning glance sweep over us, we ceased our ruminations and extended our sincere expressions of welcome to the newcomer.

In the next few days, Isolde's office was swamped with calls from senior managers demanding eye-to-eye meetings with the Chairman so they could ask why this chit of a girl, with no experience of the company - indeed, of any commercial company - should be preferred to them. Hector argued, rather lamely, that since this was a new post, past experience was not relevant. The circuit design office, stirred by their staff representative, (the successor to Ursula Blanchard), passed a resolution to the effect that although they welcomed the appointment of a female to the Board, they were gravely disappointed that one of the company's current senior female managers, or even one of their own number, had not been so appointed; and to emphasise their dismay, they would, from the following Monday, and for a period of five working days, work strictly to the terms of their formal contracts. (This resulted in some of them working far harder than they intended or were accustomed to).

As I expected, the surface tension died away after a few days. The more quiescent of the staff shrugged and accepted that if the boss wanted to appoint this strange anaemic creature to a non-job, then that was his business; but there was still a bottled-up feeling of resentment amongst many EGCol employees. One day, when I was discussing possible organisation changes with Hector, he confided in me.

"You know why I put Grace on the Board, don't you?"

"I must confess I don't," I said. "It's as much a mystery to me as it is to the other staff."

"It's her purity, you see, her purity! It's a unique quality, unique, far more rare than all those pedestrian virtues of experience, track record and dogged endeavour."

"That's all very well, boss," I said, "but what is she actually going to do?"

"It is she who will identify what we have to do to bring Goodness into the world. She will find the path and we will follow."

"Oh, really, boss!" I protested. "You're not still brooding about all that nonsense that Ursula Blanchard was on about, are you? Surely you must have realised that was merely her attempt..."

"I know all about her attempt. But no matter how sordid her motive, she was unconsciously inspired and spoke the truth. I'm convinced of it!"

"You do realise, don't you," I said, "that there is still a lot of resentment about the appointment. Some of the staff wonder whether you have lost your judgement."

"I know, I know!" groaned Hector. "But how can I recover my credibility? I can't go back and take her off the Board again; and I can't hide her away and hope people will forget all about her."

"The way to regain your people's faith in you," I advised, "is to take on a powerful adversary and defeat him in single combat."

"Eh? What do you mean... single combat?"

"I've had one of my dreams," I said. "You had gone across to Brittany at the head of your troops..."

"Wait a minute," interrupted Hector. "What's all this about 'head of my troops'? You're talking rubbish!"

I continued without explanation (it's an exasperating habit we seers have). "... head of your troops and landed in St Malo. Whilst there you heard about a fearsome giant who lived in a cave and terrorised the countryside around. He ate the young children, raped all the maidens and killed all the young heroes who set out to save them. But you were undaunted and went forth, quite alone, to his cave, picking your way amongst the bones of your predecessors strewn along the way; then you engaged the giant in a terrible and bloody battle and eventually emerged victorious to the boundless gratitude of the populace."

"What utter nonsense!" spluttered Hector. "Giants, caves, rapes, cannibalism... Have you been at the funny mushrooms again? And what has all this rigmarole to do with my particular problems?"

I touched my finger to my lips. "Mark by words!" I uttered mysteriously and slid quietly away.

I had had no such dream, of course. But I had learned from my network of informants that the great tycoon, Josef Teck, (who, incidentally was of grotesquely huge dimensions), was keen to acquire EGCol and absorb it into his already over-inflated business empire. Hector didn't learn of this looming threat until the news broke on the Cable TV financial channel - three days after our conversation.

Hector sought my advice.

"I can't improve on the old military dictum," I said. "The best defence is attack. Take the initiative - beard him in his den."

"Be sensible!" protested Hector "How can I possibly attack? I can't take over his business - it's a hundred times bigger than mine, and he knows it. I would be ridiculed."

"You don't have to pretend to take over his entire empire," I said. "He has so many fingers in so many pies that there's bound to be a product or service of his which your company uses. Identify it and attack that."

Round One went to Hector. He found that of the many modems used in the links interconnecting the Boskey Common head office with the regional offices, some were made by one of Teck's subsidiary companies. A thorough check was made of the reliability and transmission efficiency of these models and there was soon enough data to carry out a regression analysis and demonstrate, to Hector's satisfaction, that the items were not meeting the specified performance parameters. He sent a voicegram to Teck demanding a meeting to discuss the matter. Teck's first reaction to so trivial an issue was to refer Hector to the MD of the small company that manufactured the items; then he recollected his ambition to acquire EGCol and decided it might be advantageous to meet the young fellow in person. He replied with a voicegram inviting Hector to lunch...

... (Round Two to Teck) aboard his luxury yacht moored off St Malo. Teck's private helicopter would be sent to bring Hector on board and then take him home again after the meeting. Hector asked me whether he should go and which of his directors should go with him in support. "Go alone!" I urged. "Don't forget - single combat!"

Hector was duly lifted on to the yacht and arrived fifteen minutes before lunchtime. He was met by the on-board butler.

"Mr Teck presents his apologies," he intoned, "but he is in the communications room giving an interview to Russian television. He shouldn't be very long. Meanwhile, do have a drink. We have some rather rare American whiskies."

Ten minutes later, Hector, inexperienced in any type of whisky, let alone twenty-five year Old Kentucky Moonbeam, had become gently stoned; then Josef Teck appeared.

"Don't trouble to get up," the great man boomed, to Hector's relief. "I'm terribly sorry to have kept you waiting. I have just been interviewed by Russia's Economics TV Channel and they have been so interested in what I have had to say, in Russian, about solving that poor benighted country's problems that they would like me to say it all over again for the other members of the Euro/Asian Federation. Russian isn't the first language in some of those countries so I'll just have to give my spiel again in Kazhak, Uzbechistani and Kirghiz. Don't wait lunch for me. I'll catch up."

(Round Three to Teck).

The uneasy movements of the yacht at its moorings combined with the effects of Old Moonbeam were, by this time, making Hector feel very uneasy indeed. He had just enough presence of mind to dive into his brief-case and extract Elaine's computerised cure-all, SCABBARD. Clutching at the last vestiges of self-control, he shakily typed in 'Feeling Sick' and clapped the pads to his temples. Within a few minutes his symptoms had disappeared and his appetite had grown sharp and lusty, so he was well into his dessert before Teck strode in again. The great tycoon sank into his chair like an airship settling into its hangar and sonorously ingested a large bowl of soup; a young tuna, well grilled in mustard, followed without delay, and was chased down into Teck's cavernous digestive depths by a buttock of venison accompanied by many side-bowls of vegetables and a palate-cleansing rainbow of sorbets. Hector was still sipping his coffee and thinking he would have to describe this meal to Mark's food research team and Teck was engaging a huge chunk of suppurating Stilton, before the business discussion began.

"So, dear boy, you don't like my company's modems," belched Teck. "What do you propose to do about it?"

"If you look at these data," said Hector, dipping into his brief-case...

"I've seen all the data I want to see," interrupted Tech, puffing at a missile-sized cigar "Let's not waste time on facts. You know as well as I do that you can prove whatever you like with them. I asked you what you propose to do about it."

"Our supply-and-maintain contract with your company expires in two months' time," said Hector, trying to sound composed and masterful, "and I do not propose to renew it."

"Since your modem business is as about as important to me as a gnat's bollock," roared Teck, dipping into a tankard of vintage port, "I can't see myself losing much sleep over that!"

"Ah, but think of the negative PR!" Hector quickly thrust in. "What about the loss of prestige to your business as a whole! The media would say you were losing your grip."

Teck laughed so loud the deck shook beneath him. "You seem to forget, young man, that I own most of the media. I don't care a tinker's fart what they think privately. They publish what I tell them... no, no, I shouldn't say that, should I?... it's well-known they have complete editorial freedom... they publish whatever I gently hint would please me to see published."

He delicately picked at his teeth with a fish-fork. "However, we might come to an arrangement which could be mutually advantageous.

Suppose you bought into my modem company: you could then have a say on the design and performance of the product. And then I would have a little extra cash to buy into something else - your helium balloon business, for example. Big smiles all round!"

"It's worth considering," replied Hector, "but if I bought into your modem company I would want 75.1 per cent of the equity."

"Oho!" roared Teck. "Going to replace me as chairman, are you? And are you going to let me become chairman of your helium balloon business?"

"The question doesn't arise," replied Hector blandly. "It's not a separate company: it's one of corporate EGCol's many ventures. In any case, all my company's activities have a strictly ethical foundation. Forgive me for saying so, but you have the reputation of being utterly ruthless and totally without scruples. I can't see you fitting into EGCol's scheme of things."

This remark stung Teck (so Round Four to Hector). He had long passed the stage when monetary gain had any meaning for him: for several years his principal interest lay in the sheer delight of winning a contest in acquisition. But even that was beginning to pall: he was now entering a phase when expanding the boundaries of his great empire had lost its relish and had been replaced by a desire to be acknowledged by the Establishment as an outstanding contributor to the nation's well-being. (Our nation, that is; his original nation had long since been extinguished).

"I'm sorry to hear you say that," he said mournfully. "I may have cut a few corners in my youth but those days are far behind me. I'm a solid citizen now, boosting exports to every continent under the sun, sponsoring sporting events that promote the brotherhood of nations and contributing - strictly incognito, of course - to a whole heap of charities. And I'm equally keen to do my bit for the Arts." His eyes flickered direct to Hector's. "You've got your feet well stuck into the Arts, haven't you?"

In a momentary flash Hector sensed that a line was being held out to him... but did it end in a baited hook or a message for help? Whatever it was, he must grab it and play it.

"I'm proud to say," he asserted, "that the arts festivals in Boskey Common have now received international recognition. No less a person than Princess Ruby of Transylvania will be visiting us in two week's time because she has heard that a noted figure in the world of ballet has joined my staff. It is well known that the Princess's main ambition in life is to form a ballet company bearing her name and she will be seeking my advice on how to do so. Unfortunately, I will have to inform Her Highness that establishing a ballet or opera company is an extremely expensive undertaking : it ruined some of the most prominent public figures of the twentieth century."

Teck leaned forward. "Princess Ruby is a close friend of King Harry, isn't she?"

"So it is rumoured," said Hector coldly, as though such tittle tattle was beneath him.

Teck's nose was now almost touching Hector's. "I'll tell you what I am prepared to do," his voice dropped to a conspiratorial rumble. "I'll let you buy more than 76 percent of my modem company at market prices and you can assume control. In return, when Princess Ruby visits you and mentions her desire to form her own ballet company - which, you assure me, she will - you will tell her that you have been authorised by me personally to say that I would be proud to provide all the financial backing that would be needed for such a magnificent venture. Naturally, I would remain in the shadows, but if she had the opportunity to mention the part I had played to King Harry - not too ostentatiously of course, just sort of, in passing - then that would be sufficient reward. It would be EGCol's responsibility to find the dancers, musicians, technicians, in short, the entire company; oh, and also to stage a magnificent gala performance on the company's first night."

"At which you would be present."

"At which I would be present."

"Seated at the right hand of Princess Ruby?"

"Since you insist."

Hector reflected for a few moments. He had just the right people on his staff to form such a company; he couldn't form it in its full glory in time for Princess Ruby's visit, of course, but the Borealis Company, with some augmentation, could be its nucleus and be sufficient to demonstrate that a start had been made. At the same time he could be seen to have taken control of a part (albeit a very small part) of the Teck empire. He grunted assent and held out his hand to be engulfed, crushed and shaken in the tycoon's ham-like fist.

(Round Five and Contest to Hector).

When Hector returned to his office the next day he was so badgered by directors, managers and staff about what had happened in St Malo and what Teck was like that he closed the office thirty minutes earlier than usual and gave an informal presentation in the Board Room. The place was so packed that there were people sitting on the great oval table. Properly diffident, Hector described the events of the previous day (omitting unnecessary and confusing detail, such as the American whisky) and told how he had not only virtually acquired control over the modem company but also had persuaded the great man to fund the creation of a brand new ballet company which would have its first world performance in the Gwendoline Theatre.

Hector turned to Grace Halliday. "This is your first major task," he said. "I want you to do no less than to build up a ballet company which will be universally accepted as being amongst, say, the top five in the world. You will, of course, be able to use your own little company as a basis but it will have to be greatly expanded and contain the finest artistes from the five continents. I don't expect you to reach that status immediately - I'm not an unreasonable man - but you should aim to be there in... er... two years. It is to be named after Princess Ruby, so right from the outset it must be worthy of Royal patronage."

Grace blushed prettily and said she would do her best. (She was confident of success: after all, she knew a great deal about the ballet world... and wasn't her uncle one of the best business organisers in the country?)

The meeting concluded in a patter of polite applause. Hector was on form again: his appointment of this strange virginal creature had been vindicated and he had, so it seemed, triumphed in single combat over a giant.

CHAPTER TEN

But it wasn't all unsullied happiness and progress in those days; we had our share of sadness and tragedy. One of Fate's victims, I'm sorry to say, was Isolde, Hector's Personal Assistant.

She was a lovely Irish girl (I expect you have noticed how so often beauty attracts disaster) with the full Irish complement of dark hair, blue eyes and magnolia complexion. At the time of this story she had been with Hector for about eighteen months and was twenty four years old. Although she was subjected to the full range of his moods, from dark introspection to schoolboy jocosity, she remained unruffled and serene, protecting him from outside distractions when he was in a manic creative phase, or assembling his correspondence, staff and visitors into an orderly sequence when he seemed capable of straightforward administration. Her competence and steadfastness were greatly valued by Hector and the Board of Directors; she was particularly valued by Mark, the Director of Marketing.

Mark's wife had, unhappily, died from the side effects of an anti-pregnancy drug before he joined our company and he clearly missed her greatly; in fact, we had assumed that he had been so deeply affected by her loss that he would remain single for the rest of his life. But it soon became obvious to everyone who visited the directors' floor and Hector's outer office that Mark had been smitten by Isolde's beauty and lost no opportunity to call in her office or summon her to his. Isolde didn't reciprocate this infatuation: indeed, she was conscious of the fifteen years difference in their ages and was embarrassed by his attentions. She must have said something to this effect to her brother, Rory, when he was visiting her from Ireland, because one day Rory appeared in an excitable state at the EGCol building and demanded to see Mark. The ensuing quarrel could be heard all over the top two floors with Rory shouting that Mark was far too old for his sister and that he was not to lay a finger upon her. Poor Isolde was more embarrassed than ever Just to add to the commotion, Mark's seventeen year old nephew, Tarquin, arrived, saying the had been invited by his uncle to see the advanced technological facilities of the office. Hearing his uncle's voice raised in terror, he rushed into Mark's office to see Rory about to brain him with a work-station keyboard. Tarquin rushed in between them and gave Rory a mighty shove. Rory somersaulted backwards over Mark's desk and thudded into a tangle heap with an explosive 'crack!'; his arm had been broken. Tarquin hadn't escaped damage either: the keyboard he had deflected from his uncle had caught him a heavy blow on the temple and had laid him out unconscious. By now a few of the other directors - and all the secretaries - had arrived and were beginning to sort out the injured. Rory was carried downstairs and was loaded into a cable-ambulance, Mark was mopped down and restored to his chair behind his desk and Tarquin, still unconscious, was carried into Isolde's office. Hector had heard the commotion and emerged to find out what was going on. Isolde, apparently perfectly composed, briefly explained the situation and politely requested the use of his computerised cure-all kit, SCABBARD. Hector hesitated - he didn't like others taking advantage of something designed specifically for him - and then relented. Isolde typed in the word 'concussed' and applied the pads to Tarquin's temples; within a few minutes he shook his head and opened his eyes. His first vision was of Isolde bending over him. Need I say more?

It was at about this time that I was trying to extend my information-gathering network to the north coast of Brittany to keep tabs on Josef Teck's activities. I had had to depend on Hector himself for my earlier account of his encounter with the great tycoon; but now that there had been an initial exchange of fire, so to speak, it became important to know what was going on in the Teck camp when Hector wasn't there. Old-fashioned bugs introduced into his yacht's communications equipment or hidden behind the El Greco in the stateroom would never do; he employed the most sophisticated of debugging systems. Eventually I hit upon the idea of renting a seaman's cottage on the headland and installing inside it an enormous acoustic horn of the type used in the 1930's for detecting the approach of aircraft. From this I could pick up a rich jumble of sounds emerging from Teck's yacht (the QM III), embracing the whine of its motors, the chatter of the crew, the clatter of plates in the galley and, of course, the sonorous boom of Teck himself. This is where the clever part came in: from numerous television and radio recordings of Teck's speeches and interviews I had composed an accurate voiceprint, as unique to Teck as his fingerprints. From this, I got one of the lads in EGCol's laboratory to design and construct a quartz crystal filter which permitted Teck's voice, and Teck's voice alone, to go through; all other sounds were rejected. It was then an easy matter to use SAD (small aperture dish) satellite communications to relay Teck's utterances back to my little monitoring station in Boskey Common.

One day, whilst I was working on the equipment in the tumbledown seaman's cottage, a young man, handsome in looks but mournful in expression, presented himself to me. He handed me a cassette which I jacked into my work-station. Mark's face appeared on the screen: "Hallo, Melvyn," it said, "let me introduce you to my nephew, Tarquin. He's touring all EGCol's offices and out-stations to get an overview of the company's activities. I would be very glad if you could take him under your wing for the next few weeks. I'm sure he will be very useful to you in your present work - whatever that may be. Thanks." (Did I detect a touch of sarcasm in that last sentence?) Well, as it happened, I was quite glad to have an extra pair of hands. Young Tarquin worked hard and was really helpful but nothing would shift his hang-dog expression. I tried to extract the cause of his melancholy, but he would say nothing.

Then, one day, Tarquin, being nearest to the beastly thing, answered a call on the international viewphone. It was Isolde, intending to ask me something on Hector's behalf about company law. She was delighted and astonished when she saw who it was at the other end of the connection.

"Hello! It's Tarquin!" she cried. "I wondered where on earth you had gone to. I have a business query to put to Melvyn but when that's over perhaps we could have a brief chat."

Tarquin mumbled and stumbled back over his heels in vacating his chair for me. I dealt with the question and then pushed the youth back in front of the instrument. Tarquin's attempt to conduct a conversation was pitiful to see: he stammered and gurgled, went through a range of facial contortions and colours and alternated between short bursts of rapid speech and long periods of embarrassed silence. Although Isolde, so much more mature, was in control of her conversation, it was clear that she was deeply affected as well. They were just reaching a period of verbal intimacy - I was preparing to tip-toe from the room - when we saw the door of Isolde's office open and Mark stride in. He stopped short when he recognised Tarquin's face on Isolde's screen, then stepped forward and switched off the connection.

Ho! Ho! I thought. So that's why young Tarquin has been sent to help me!

We had no more messages from Isolde (she had been forbidden to send any) although most of the other PAs and secretaries called each day in the normal line of business. Tarquin became more and more miserable and announced, when my installation and testing work had been completed, that he was going off on his own to explore the world. I lent him my food ioniser, warned him not to get close to other persons of any sex without first checking their aura on a waveform analyser, and waved him a fond farewell. Soon afterwards I returned to Boskey Common; I could see that poor Isolde was going into decline. To her it seemed that Tarquin had vanished without leaving his personal EM location number Mark was taking every opportunity to - as they used to say - 'press his suit' and Isolde was beginning to wilt under the constant pressure; she even seemed to be responding just a little to his advances. Truly it is said that man's most powerful weapon in courtship is unflagging persistence.

Things went on like this for several months until one day - great excitement - a call came through from Tarquin; he was in the Vatican

City. (The Vatican had become a private company in 2010 AD. It had squandered vast sums of money to fashionable artists for paintings which had rapidly crumbled and faded, owing to the inferior quality of both the paints and the painters. Consequently, it fetched only a knock-down price when it was bought by a Venezuelan oil company which greatly prized the City's world-wide communications network and the sway it still had over tens of millions of simple South American folk. The Pope had become, in effect, the Group MD of a multinational company but he and his regional MDs [i.e. cardinals] still retained their quaint costumes for those festivals when tourists were certain to be in attendance). Tarquin was calling because he had had an idea for a business venture which seemed to be both profitable and ethical - a natural candidate for EGCol's portfolio.

Unfortunately both Hector and Lance were out of the office so Tarquin was connected through to Mark.

"Nice to hear from you again," lied Mark. "What can I do for you?"

Tarquin was discomforted at being confronted by his uncle. He could still recall the image of Mark striding across Isolde's office and disrupting their intimate viewphone conversation. But, as he had no reason to doubt his uncle's loyalty to EGCol, he proceeded to outline his plan.

"This was a bit before my time, uncle," he said, "but do you remember back in the last century there was a lot of worry about deforestation and the destruction of the rain forests?"

"I was but a lad at the time," said Mark, "but I remember the problem being discussed."

"As usual," went on Tarquin, "the pendulum swung the other way. All the newspaper proprietors - some of the greatest users of wood pulp - undertook to have two trees planted for every one they had chopped down. Then came the virtual replacement of paper by electronic media, so all those trees planted a generation ago are now coming to maturity without any use for them. The world is now grossly over-forested - it's the single biggest threat to the world's ecological balance."

"I know, I know," said Mark wearily. "So what?"

"At the same time," persisted Tarquin, "there are still millions and millions of people in Africa and India who are starving."

There was several seconds' silence from Mark. Then:-

"What are you saying? You want them to eat trees!"

"Well, very nearly. I've been working during the last few weeks with an American company that has established itself in Vatican City as a tax haven. It has engineered an organic reagent that can convert wood pulp into a substance that is rich in protein and sugar and has the appearance and consistency of yogurt. There's a magnificent opportunity for EGCol here. You could arrange for the new growth of trees to be chopped down again - much to the thanks of ecologists - have them pulped, acquire the pulp-to-protein converter from my American friends and perhaps even carry out the transformation to yogurt brickettes during the journey to the point of sale."

Mark was silent, incredulous, for a moment. Then:-

"Are you sure this conversion process works?"

"I'm certain! I've seen it carried out in the laboratory."

"Sounds brilliant!" enthused Mark. "I'll certainly bring this to Hector's attention and to the rest of the Board... giving you full credit, of course."

"Thanks, uncle."

"Oh," continued Mark, smiling darkly to himself, 'there's a little bit of personal news that might interest you. It would be in order for you to congratulate me."

"Oh, really. Why? What's happened?"

"I'm engaged to Isolde. We're being married in two weeks' time."

(He wasn't, of course).

Mark enjoyed the explosive silence for a few moments and discontinued the connection.

Mark did present the scheme to the EGCol Board of Directors but omitted to mention Tarquin's creative initiative. Isolde was forbidden to contact Tarquin in the Vatican and all calls from the Vatican were put through to Mark. So poor Tarquin didn't know the project had been approved, didn't know the Board was unaware of his contribution and thought that Isolde had become Mark's wife; and she was still wishing, hoping, praying that she could see him again. They both tried to blunt their sorrows by overworking. Tarquin had obtained a permanent position in the American Chemical Company and had been noticed by the Managing Director, Dr Fischer, as being a bright and ambitious young man with potential for a senior management post. Americans still clung to the concept that the family was an integral part of the business organisation, so Tarquin was invited to the MD's home to 'meet the folks'. His good looks, charm and lively intelligence won the affection of the MD's wife, son and daughter - particularly the daughter - and he soon became a frequent and favoured guest. So, there were these two young people, both away from their natural habitat, their blood and other vital juices stirred by the hot Italian summer sun, thrust into each other's company... What more natural an outcome than lust? And when autumn had succeeded summer and the blood and other vital juices had cooled down a little, what more inevitable than lust condensing into love? By the way, the young lady's name was also Isolde. Coincidence, eh?

So Tarquin married Isolde II and Mark allowed this particular item of joyful news to reach the ears of Isolde I. He was hoping that this would spur her to throw herself into his arms but she became even more despondent and listless: so much so that even Hector, who was usually unaware of the physical and mental health of the people around him... even Hector noticed his PA's pitiful condition and asked her for an explanation. Isolde refused counselling interviews at first, but after a week or two, wanting a shoulder to cry on, she told the sad story of her love for Tarquin, his banishment from the EGCol office, the interrupted viewphone conversation and his apparent disappearance; and now... the last twist in the wound, the news that he had married the daughter of an American chemical engineer, located in the Vatican. It was this last item that jolted Hector's attention: was this not the very company that Mark had recommended as a partner in the trees-to-yogurt venture?

Hector questioned the communications-receptionist, who, like every other female in the office was fully aware of Isolde's passion for Tarquin and who remembered the excitement when he called from Vatican City; she also recalled that Hector and Lance had been out that day so the call had been put through to Mark and that Mark had terminated the conversation before Isolde had had a chance to have a few words and sighs with her beloved. Hector then inspected the Marketing Department's job number records and could find none that corresponded to preliminary work on the wood-pulp project: it had apparently been snatched by Mark out of the thin air. The implication was clear: Mark had stolen Tarquin's idea and had interfered in his love-life as well. Hector was furious; Mark was sacked.

Meanwhile, back in Vatican City, Tarquin had been made product manager of Project Woodyog. His energy was boundless: he badgered the R&D Department further to refine the reagent so that all traces of bark, knots and splinters could be eradicated, he drove the production department frantic in building up the assembly of autoclaves needed for full-scale manufacture and he personally designed the logo to be printed on the final pots and brickettes. He had to admit, however, that the product was not very palatable: there was a lingering flavour of sawdust. So every day he tried out new additives - fruits, liqueurs, herbs - and ate the stuff with every meal. After four weeks of this regime he became terribly ill; none of the local doctors could diagnose the malady because it was quite novel - he had virtually invented it himself - but some thought it had affinities with Dutch elm disease.

Tarquin took to his bed and became more gnarled with each day that passed. His father-in-law, Dr Fischer, contacted Hector in desperation to see whether there was anything EGCol could do. At my advice, Hector, again a little reluctantly, brought out SCABBARD, and put it into Isolde I's hands. Who better to entrust it to? "Go!" he said. "Take this and my personal cable-car and speed to Tarquin in Vatican City.

This is probably his last hope."

The news reached the carers around Tarquin's bedside that help was on its way; but Isolde II, although deeply anguished by her husband's illness, was consumed with jealousy. Why should this woman from England be sent to attend to him when she, his wife, was already at his bedside? During his third day in bed Tarquin's face began to swell and crack so that he was afire with pain and could scarcely speak. He managed to utter a few words to his wife. "Go to the top of St. Peter's," he whispered, "and look out for Hector's cable-car. It's very distinctive - it's covered in black and gold stripes." Isolde II went away but she didn't climb to the top of St. Peter's; she sat outside one of Rome's many cafes drinking gin-fizzes and seething with anger. When it was dusk she returned to her husband's bedside. "Any sign?" he croaked. She shook her head "None!" (In fact, Isolde I, in Hector's own car, had already passed through the Rome toll-gate and was whizzing along the last line to Vatican City).

Tarquin's body was becoming stiff and cold. He tried to rub some life into his legs but he couldn't move his arms or fingers; he seemed to be dividing into laminated slices; one cheek burst open like slashed bark, emitting a slow dark resin. Just then the cluster of people round his bedside heard a shrill commotion in the corridor. The door crashed open and Isolde I burst in with the titanium case in her arms; she looked vainly round the room for her lover. "Where's...where's Tarquin?" she cried. Fingers pointed to the unrecognisable log lying in the bed. Isolde I shrieked and fell senseless across the body; and Isolde II, suddenly realising she had killed her husband by refusing to give him the last vestige of hope, slumped from her chair in a dead faint.

So that's what love can do. It killed Tarquin, one of the brightest and most beautiful young men it has been my privilege to see; and it despatched the two lovely Isoldes into gibbering lunacy for ever and ever.

CHAPTER ELEVEN

Although Grace Halliday's own taste in ballet stopped short at the Tchaikovsky/Petipa romantic classics, she realised she would have to produce a novelty for the gala performance in the presence of Princess Ruby, so she decided to choreograph the piece herself. After a week of tortured brainstorming she hit upon the idea of a young virgin of impeccable purity (i.e. Grace) being assailed by each of the seven deadly sins in turn and emerging unscathed from their attentions; the action would take place in some great city with each scenelet being set in a district appropriate to the sin being exercised. For a time it worried her that she envisaged each of the sins being personified by a male dancer and that she would be the only female on the stage; but what must be, must be.

During the period of intensive rehearsals and preparations for the Princess's visit I was monitoring the QMIII and Josef Teck's utterances. Much of this was of purely local administrative interest - orders for vast quantities of food and drink from around the world, bids for major works of art, and the purchase of presents for his concubines; (this was no light task for his procurer because Teck liked to have at least one odalisque from each racial group). However, some of this intercepted information was of concern to EGCol, and this I extracted and passed on to Hector. Amongst other things we learned that Teck intended to upstage Hector in the eyes of the Princess by wearing a gold lamé costume. It was being built - no doubt with expressions of refined distaste - by a well-known firm of tailors in Saville Row who were to dispatch it to him in his own cable-car two days before the performance. As it zoomed over the Channel I gave it a quick blast from my old moon-bounce transmitter so that when Teck eagerly opened the boxes on the QMIII he found that his costume had melted: quite fetching in a Daliesque kind of way, but not what he had wanted. He had to make do with his workaday light grey tropicals with the silver thread insets.

Hector had entrusted Lance and Gwendoline with the preparations for Princess Ruby's visit and was pleased to see how well they collaborated together They decided that as soon as the Princess's cable-car touched down on Charlie's Fields she would be greeted by a party of small children playing her national anthem ('Big Bang, it is of thee') on a variety of synthesisers and electronic generators. Whilst listening to this with an expression of surprised delight she would be greeted by Hector and Gwendoline and then whisked off to a VIP lounge where she would be plied with refreshing beverages. Then would come a tour of the artists' colony where the more picturesque inhabitants could be seen at their crafts and be heard singing their age-old worksongs. The evening would conclude with a magnificent banquet in Dromdeal Tower. (Food was a problem: Hector realised that flavoured pabulum, the normal fare of Boskeyites, would be inappropriate for an occasion of this magnificence. Unfortunately, the EGCol laboratories had not yet perfected their creation of synthetic sausage, egg and bacon; so Josef Teck kindly agreed to supply the victuals).

The second day was filled with more visits: to the childrens' creche where the toddlers were taught civics and skin-painting; to the EGCol Museum where the prototypes of the company's first world-beating projects - the tadpole farm machinery, the helium zeppelins and the transparent sidewalks - were on display; and then to the EGCol offices with their bewildering array of optoelectronic equipment including - still where Hector had placed it so many years ago - the crystal module which enabled them all to interact.

The climax of the second day, indeed of the whole visit, was the first performance of Grace's ballet at the Gwendoline Theatre. All of Boskey's wit and beauty was there in their best tabards and tights, wimples and ribbons. The excited buzz of conversation almost drowned the orchestra tuning up its electronic viols, serpents and shawms; and then there came a sudden hush as the spotlight picked out the entrance of the lovely Princess Ruby into the Chairman's box accompanied by Hector, Gwendoline and Teck. No-one knew how old the Princess was, but she was certainly very handsome: one could discern high cheekbones from some distant Slav antecedent, a touch of Oriental almond-eye, a rich Levantine flush in complexion and glinting Moorish tresses. Her long silver costume swept unimpeded from a choker of jade at her neck to a hem of humming-bird plumage sweeping the floor. Hector and Gwendoline seemed but insubstantial shadows in the company of the Princess's glamour and Teck's massive presence.

The programme opened with the old classic 'La Sylphide' which Grace and her company danced with their accustomed crisp elegance. The audience was pleased but their applause fell short of rapture; they had seen it all before. Teck was visibly bored: these fluttering white spirits were not to his taste. After a brief intermission, Lance Mere appeared before the curtain and made this announcement:

"Ladies and gentlemen. The work you have just seen was the last performance of the Borealis Ballet Company." [Shocked cries of 'No! No!' Dramatic pause.] "But I am now proud to announce that from the ashes of that splendid group of artistes there now springs, phoenix-like, the nucleus of a new and far grander company which we are privileged to call - with Her Royal Highness's consent - 'Princess Ruby's Royal Ballet'. I am sure you will be delighted to know that the lovely Grace Halliday will be both its artistic director and prima ballerina and that it is her aim to build the company up into one of the major forces in world theatre. That is no mean ambition and it would have been difficult - no, virtually impossible - of achievement without the financial support so generously guaranteed to us by Mr Josef Teck, who, I am happy to say, is with us here this evening." [A spotlight picks out Teck's huge head; he responds with a graceful inclination].

"Tonight is a great night in the annals of theatrical history for we are about to see the world premiere of the first ballet specifically created for this new company. Ladies and gentlemen - The Seven Deadly Sins."

The stage darkens; deep brooding music from the serpents and bass viols is pierced by lightening-like flashes from the flageolets. A pale blue sky appears out of the darkness and outlines in silhouette the towers and ziggurats of a great city. The cliff-like face of the buildings is illuminated by a back-projection depiction of a superior shopping area (perhaps Bond St. or Burlington Arcade?) Grace dances in, entirely in white, one white lily in her hair. Shop windows spring into activity with snake-hipped salesmen competing to display their jewels, furs and fine clothes. At first she dances by blithely, hiding her face from these temptations; but the salesmen redouble their efforts, brandishing their worldly treasures more and more extravagantly; she hesitates, weakens, makes to take the lily from her headband in payment... when there is a crash from the orchestra, a brilliant white light encompassing a tiny red cross appears over the city and the undefiled virgin pushes aside the supplicants and dances away into the distance. Blackout.

In the next scene we are in some great banqueting hall (could it be The Mansion House or Guildhall?) and a dais is peopled by a slowly moving frieze of be-robed and be-wigged grand personages. Grace slides in, haughtily erect and dances a stately pas-de-deux with each dignitary in turn, each partner miming homage and submission. The grandest grandee of all attempts to place a jewelled circlet on her brow in place of the lily and... crash!, the orchestra cries out again, the light appears scorching the beamed roof, the dignitaries shrink into rodents and scuttle away and Grace's body bends from proud convexity into modest girlish pliancy.

In this manner Covetousness and Pride were followed by Sloth (set in the bed department in a furniture store in Tottenham Court Road), Gluttony (the food hall in Harrods), Envy (a royal procession down the Mall), Wrath (a brawl in an East End drinking den) and Lust (a worm-heap of writhing pimps in Soho). In each case the lily was about to be snatched from her head when the blinding light would appear accompanied by an orchestral tumult. After the last triumph over a sin (that of Lust), the heavenly light appeared to grow larger and larger, the music became increasingly radiant, the skyline of London sank towards the ground and Grace, gliding with infinite elegance, floated across the rooftops to be absorbed in the effulgence. Final triumphal chords from the orchestra. Curtain. Thunderous applause.

Keith Kendall was sitting next to Lance Mere in the front row.

"Where on earth did she get the ideas for the right areas in London for the sins?" he asked. "She's never been in London in her life."

"I told her" said Lance.

"And what about all those erotic gestures and gropings in the Lust sequence?"

"I taught her those, too."

The select audience up in the Chairman's box were as impressed as the groundlings down below. Princess Ruby made it graciously known she would like to meet Grace and the company so the royal group made its way behind the stage where Grace and her seven male dancers were already drawn up in obsequious file. The Princess fluttered her eyelashes at each of the ballerins in turn and then spoke long and earnestly to Grace in her excellent but accented English. She thanked Grace for forming a company in her name and hoped it would indeed blossom into a majestic ensemble of hundreds of artistes and have an extensive repertoire. Teck was even more effusive. He crushed Grace in a mighty bear-hug, and when she was released, tottering like an emergent butterfly, he grasped her thin hands in his massive paw and covered them in slobbering kisses.

"Marvellous! Marvellous!" he kept on saying. "I must congratulate you, my dear. Never seen anything like it. A masterpiece!"

He's going over the top a bit, I thought. He'll scare poor little Grace out of her wits. Or is this his version of seductive fore-play? Has he run out of Anglo-Saxon concubines? But, no, to be fair, I believe he was really moved by the performance. It was probably the first work of art he had seen that he couldn't buy and install in the stateroom of his yacht.

After the composer, set designer, costumier, conductor, orchestra leader and all the other minor, but no doubt worthy, functionaries had had their thirty seconds of splendour with the Princess, the principals (i.e. the Princess, Teck, Hector, Gwendoline, Grace and me) quaffed New Mexican champagne. (The French vineyards had, once again, been devastated by phylloxera). Hector, having included me in this august company, introduced me to the guests as 'adviser and guru'. Princess Ruby was very gracious towards me but Teck glared at me suspiciously Downing champagne by the tankard without any discernible effect, he went into a series of physical manoeuvres to keep the Princess and Grace within his frontal arc whilst presenting the vast planes of his back to Hector, Gwendoline and me.

"As you know, dear ladies," he was saying, "I came here tonight with the intention of funding the Princess Ruby ballet to be amongst the finest in the world. But now I want to go further. I want your company to travel the world, to be seen in and revered by London, Paris, Rome, Barcelona, St. Petersburg, Moscow, New York, Tokyo, Rio..."

"Perth, Australia?" Hector suggested irreverently from behind his back.

"Pretoria, South Africa?" I added helpfully.

Teck turned and snarled. "Let us not be facetious!"

"But sir," interjected Grace quietly, re-engaging his attention, "that will add immensely to the expense of the operation. Think of all the logistical problems involved in moving all the instruments, costumes, scenery... not to mention dancers, musicians, regisseurs, physiotherapists..."

"Don't bother your head about such matters!" boomed Teck. "You look after the artistry and leave all the practical matters to me."

"You really are most generous, Mr Teck," said Princess Ruby in a husky velvet voice, her orbs glowing like headlights in a fog. "I will most certainly let my dear friend, King Harry, know how so very helpful you have been."

"My inestimable pleasure!" bowed Teck.

And so a small provincial dance troupe suddenly blossomed overnight into the nucleus of a major company of high international status.

Well, potentially.

CHAPTER TWELVE

A few days after Tarquin's tragic death Hector despatched James Perceval to Vatican City to arrange for the young man's body to be brought back to his native soil and to do what he could to comfort Isolde; whilst there, he was to discontinue the development contract with GenCo, the America/Vatican company with whom Tarquin had been working. Comforting Isolde was the most difficult task of all: she was in a catatonic state, alternating long periods of rigid inactivity with terrifying bouts of violent destruction. All Perceval could do was to install her in a large psychiatric hospital on the shore of Lake Constance and undertake that EGCol would pay for her care and attention for as long as she would stay there. As it happened, Dr Rex Fischer, the Chief Executive of GenCo, sent his deranged daughter, Isolde II, there, as well.

At the next meeting of Hector and the Board round the great oval table, Perceval recounted the melancholy tale of the last days of Tarquin and his two Isoldes. This was the gloomiest Board meeting I had attended, made all the more unsettling by the vacant place where Mark had once sat. Perceval, having concluded his report on the star-crossed lovers, then went on to say:

"However, there is one item of news which, after this sad interlude, I hope you will find more positive. As you know, I was instructed by you, Chairman, to bring to an end the rather loose contractual arrangements we had with GenCo relating to the wood-pulp-yogurt project. I had no difficulty in accomplishing this: Dr Fischer was as saddened as we have been by the death of Tarquin and, of course, his own daughter's breakdown. He felt he had to accept much of the responsibility for Tarquin's terrible fate; but I tried to comfort him by saying that Tarquin was also to blame for dosing himself so frequently with a new product and so recklessly with untried additives.

"Although Dr Fischer had assumed, as I had, that there would be no further relationship between our companies after this tragic episode, he was a gracious host and undertook to show me round his establishment. I should first tell you that his premises are where the old formal Vatican gardens used to be. The whole area has been bull-dozed flat and then laid with a covering of pebbles raked into geometrical patterns like a Japanese Buddhist garden. On to this base they have constructed a series of octagonal wooden buildings interlinked by walkways made from planking; these are just wide enough for Fischer to propel himself along in his battery-powered chair (the poor fellow has been crippled for some years).

"Whenever GenCo employees, of whatever age or status, have a viable idea for a new product, they are allotted one of the octagonal buildings together with a small team of supporting scientists and laboratory technicians and enough money to fund the development for two years. If, at the end of that time, the market potential seems promising and the product has passed all its safety tests then financial projections are carried out to see if they exceed the company's acceptability levels; only then is full-scale production authorised. Tarquin had been in charge of one such team, but, as you will have guessed, was too headstrong to have obeyed the company's safety procedures.

"I saw one product under development which looked if it might be of particular interest to us. It was a drug which appeared to reduce aggression to negligible levels and to foster emotions of affection and mutual assistance. I saw rats breaking up parcels of food and ensuring that all the others were well-provided before starting to tuck in themselves. I saw agile young chimpanzees climb to the tops of trees, pluck a bunch of bananas and then distribute the fruit amongst the elderly, disabled and otherwise disadvantaged of their tribe. You have all seen films of the noisy and vicious fighting which breaks out amongst animals when they dispute the possession of food: but the subjects of GenCo's drug remained quiet and peaceable."

"There is nothing new in reducing aggression," interrupted Hector. "Lobotomy and lobectomy techniques date back to the middle of the last century. They certainly reduced violent behaviour but they changed lively and intelligent people into placid zombies. What were the consequences of GenCos' drugs?"

"As far as I could gather," replied Perceval, "they didn't cause any mental deterioration. The chimps were given various intellectual exercises during the course of their treatment - you know, working out how to extract a bag of peanuts from a three-dimensional maze, that sort of thing - and, if anything, they improved as they went along. They became kindlier and brighter."

Lance joined the discussion. "This is all very well," he said, "but we come back to a question we have debated before. I'm sure it's desirable to reduce aggression and it's fine to be nice; but is that the same as being good? And, if I'm not mistaken, it's goodness that the Chairman wants us to find and propagate."

"Quite right," assented Hector.

"I thought I'd covered that point," returned Perceval," by observing that the creatures under test were not only less aggressive than formerly but that they shared out their goods with others before satisfying themselves. If that isn't goodness, what is?"

"What was GenCo's reason for developing this drug?" asked Hector.

"As is so often the case," replied Perceval, "the outcome was accidental. The company was working on a feeder additive that would increase the milk-production of nanny-goats when it was noticed that the kids of the trial goats were far less aggressive than their parents. After two generations of experimenting with goats they isolated the ingredient that was responsible for this more pacific attitude to life. They called it MAHATMA. At this stage a US government agency became interested and sent an observer as a member of the development team. It was he who suggested that the product should be upgraded to MAHATMA B - suitable for human consumption."

"Do you know why?" asked Hector.

"Dr Fischer was reluctant to go into detail," said Perceval, "but he did admit that MAHATMA B was to be introduced into the prisoners' chow in the state penitentiaries to reduce the incidence of riots."

Hector was squirming in his chair with excitement. "This is fascinating!" he enthused. "Did you express our interest in MAHATMA B? Were you able to bring some back with you?"

"MAHATMA is already outmoded," said Perceval, "and has been superseded by GRAIL (that's an acronym for Goodness, Righteousness And Ineffable Love). Yes, I did tentatively suggest that EGCol might be interested in some sort of joint venture and that I would be grateful for a small quantity of the substance for our own experimentation."

"Hang on! Hang on!" burst in Keith Kendall, in an uncharacteristic state of agitation. "Forgive me, Chairman, for this interruption, but I must say I am shocked. That lovely boy, Tarquin, has been dead scarcely a week, yet you and Perceval seem to be inclining towards another association with the very company that killed him! I'm sorry if I seem unbusinesslike, but shouldn't we feel and display some sensitivity?"

"I do understand your feelings," soothed Hector, "I assure you I do. But haven't we already established that Tarquin, poor lad, no doubt inspired to achieve something to the benefit of humanity, was rather foolish in ingesting an untested product so persistently? With this MAHATMA or GRAIL, or whatever it's called, we have an opportunity for carefully-controlled pilot tests before large-scale implementation." [He swivelled his chair to face Perceval and exclude Kendall from his field of vision]. "James, you were reporting on your attempt to obtain samples."

"Unsuccessfully I'm afraid," resumed Perceval. "Dr Fischer took what I thought was a very odd attitude to this. When I suggested you would be most grateful if I were able to take some GRAIL back with me, he said he didn't want to hurt my feelings but I wasn't the right sort of person to act as courier. You can imagine I was a bit puzzled and, to be frank, rather annoyed by this and I asked him why I was unsatisfactory He gave a very peculiar answer: he said that as far as he could tell I was a perfectly normal fellow with the usual complement of hopes and ambitions, successes and failures, merits and - perhaps - just a few blemishes and shortcomings. I agreed I was fairly normal in these respects. That, he said, was the trouble: he could only entrust GRAIL to someone of undoubted absolute purity, and such creatures were hard to find. 'What about the American prison service?' I asked. 'Were their representatives without blemish?' He winced and I then understood why he was so reluctant to tell me more about that episode. 'You're quite right,' he said, 'we did make a fundamental mistake there. Those lads certainly had their share of human frailties. That's why we had to kill off our MAHATMA; since then, not a gramme has left for the US - or, indeed, anywhere else.' So you see, Chairman, the reason why I haven't brought back any samples of GRAIL is that I'm considered not good enough to carry them!"

Hector sat biting his knuckles, twisting and turning in his big chair. The Board stared at him in silence. Then he raised his head and gave a shrill laugh.

"Of course!" he shouted. "Someone of absolute purity! Such a person is sitting here today at this very table! Our Director of Forward Planning - Grace Halliday!"

"Oh, really!" protested Kendall again. "First, we are contemplating playing a dangerous game with chemicals of doubtful provenance; and now we are thinking of sending - if you'll forgive me for saying so, Grace - an inexperienced young girl to fetch them."

"What do you say to that, Grace?" asked Hector.

Grace had not taken part in the discussion but her eyes had dilated and her cheeks had flushed when her active participation was suggested. She remained silent for a few moments then raised her great moist eyes to sweep round the table and come to rest on Hector.

"I am deeply honoured, Chairman," she said meekly, "to have this trust placed in me. I can assure the Board there is no need to worry about my safety or my inexperience of travel. I won't go alone: I'll go as artistic director and prima ballerina of a ballet company. You remember how Mr Teck encouraged us to send the Princess Ruby Company abroad, and, what's more, offered to sponsor us? Well, we can do just as he suggested and start our world tour in Rome. We can satisfy a number of objectives all at once: build up our company, have a great artistic triumph in Rome and I can slip away to meet Dr Fischer and bring back some GRAIL."

"Well said!" chortled Hector. "Oh, well said!"

Kendall shook his head. "I don't like it. I must confess I still don't like it."

(One thought struck me: there's no false modesty about our little Grace, is there? She accepts without demur that her purity is spotless and that there is no question that she, and no-one but she, should be the GRAIL-carrier But I didn't say anything).

Lance broke in. "Chairman, I agree that Grace has had a splendid idea, but I do think that a considerable degree of logistical support will be necessary. I therefore propose that I, perhaps under some fancy title such as 'regisseur', should go along as a member of the company to take charge of all the management aspects."

"I'm sure your suggestion is well-intentioned, Lance," said Hector, "but I'm afraid I can't agree. As soon as your presence was discovered - and you're a prominent personage, Lance, so it would be bound to happen - Fischer would become suspicious and pull up the drawbridge. I don't know" [roguishly] "what your lapses of virtue are, but you're sure to have had some, like everyone else, No, it has to be Grace and her company, and them alone."

He closed the meeting; his mind was made up.

When I returned to my little den I found awaiting me some messages from two of our northern provincial offices which caused me to scuttle back up to the top floor and seek an audience with Hector.

He saw me begrudgingly: he was a busy man.

"Well," he snapped, "what's all this about?"

"It relates to our Board discussion this afternoon," I said. "You know, the decision that Miss Halliday's company should visit Rome and that she should slip away and see Dr Fischer."

"Well, what about it?"

"It must be put in hand very quickly indeeed."

"Why?"

"You remember when you first took over EGCol as chairman you had some trouble from the Hadrian Group?"

"Yes. What of it?"

"I told you at the time, after we had fended them off, that they had troubles of their own which would keep them occupied for several years. That time is now up: they are trouble-free again."

"So?"

"I have information that they have also heard about GenCo's GRAIL drug and want it for themselves. They won't bother about such niceties as finding someone of infinite purity as an intermediary. They will, if necessary, take it by force."

"How do you know all this?"

"Chairman, I have these special powers..."

"Rubbish!"

"You may say 'Rubbish!' but my information is genuine. The Hadrian Group will capture GRAIL unless you move very quickly."

"But what on earth do they want it for? What good is goodness to them?"

"Chairman, don't you see the downside potential of this stuff? Feed it to one part of the population - who we will call the Goodies - and they will become non-aggressive and innocent to the point of naivete. They will become incapable of believing that everyone is not as good as themselves and so becomes easy prey to the undrugged part of humanity, the NoGoodies. Then, when the Goodies have been bled dry, you - the possessor of GRAIL - reverse the process and the old Goodies, now back to their nasty human ways again, feast upon the New Goodies (the old NoGoodies). The controllers of Goodness have the power to rob the population at large for ever. That's why Fischer is insisting that only someone of the utmost trustworthiness and purity of mind can act as a go-between. Anyone subject to normal human temptations would realise en route that something of immense commercial potential had been delivered into their hands. The ability to impose Goodness could be a terrifying force for evil."

"Aren't you equating Goodness with quiescent pacifism?" asked Hector. "There's no reason why the Goodies, as you call them, shouldn't resist hostile action by the NoGoodies."

"From what I have heard of this GRAIL stuff, boss, it quenches every form of robust physical activity, even in self-defence."

"Melvyn, I believe you're right," said Hector. "We must get the show on the road as soon as we can. Will you send Grace in to see me?"

I withdrew, passed the message on to Grace and scuttled back to my monitoring den in time to catch their conversation. Hector put the position to Grace much as I had put it to him (without, I'm afraid, giving me due credit for initiating the action) and then told her she should drop all her other activities (whatever they may be) and prepare to assemble a large company to take to Rome. He would appoint EGCol's arts impresario, Gavin Wain, to look after all the business aspects, thus leaving Grace to concentrate on building up the company from first-class dancers and musicians and to devising enough new ballets for the tour. Hector would deal direct with Josef Teck on all financial matters.

"Thank you, sir," Grace responded sweetly. "I'll get to work at once. But isn't the range of duties you propose for Mr Wain more or less the same as my uncle was offering to carry out?"

"Lance is a splendid fellow," said Hector, "and I trust him implicitly. But he is rather headstrong and I had visions of him - as soon as he had you settled in your accommodation and rehearsals were under way - I could imagine him steaming along to the Gen Co establishment and demanding to see Dr Fischer. That wouldn't do at all. These negotiations must be pursued with the utmost delicacy That is why I want you to handle Fischer with the lightest touch and to leave the day-to-day operations to Wain."

Grace nodded in understanding. Hector suppressed a sigh as he watched her slim form undulate from the room.

I had to know what was going on in Rome when the company took up residence there. But how? My moon-bounce system was far too insensitive. A small portable dish terminal could give me a satellite connection but how would the information I required get to the terminal? I reluctantly decided I had to fall back on the oldest information system of all: a spy.

During the rest of the day I kept a sharp ear and eye open on the comings and goings in Hector's office area. Mostly they were the directors and senior managers consulting him on various policy and expenditure matters, but towards the end of the day Gavin Wain was summoned to attend the Chairman's suite. Hector put on what he hoped was an encouraging smile but which turned out as a terrifying leer.

"Gavin," smiled Hector, putting on his kindly employer act, "I've been hearing things about you. You've made your mark. You're going places."

"Thank you, sir" stuttered Gavin, not sure whether this overture presaged promotion or dismissal.

"I would like to see if you are as efficient as people say you are," grinned Hector, "by assigning you to a special task. There'll be lots of hard work, responsibility and travel. How do you react to that?"

"I'm keen to show you what I can do, sir."

"Good. Well, as you know, one of our directors, Miss Grace Halliday, is forming a new ballet company which is destined to be world-famous. Very commendably, she is determined to make her mark on the artistic world as soon as she can, so she intends to launch a spectacular new season in Rome, Italy. Grace - Miss Halliday - will be working all the hours the clock gives her in forming her company and devising new works, so she will have no time for what might be called the managerial side. Do you follow me?"

"Yes, sir."

"Right, that's where you come in. You will be appointed business manager and will assume full responsibility for all details of bookings, travel, publicity, finances, front-of-the-house functions, accommodation, pay and rations, indeed, everything except the artistic side. Do you understand?"

"Er... Yes, sir."

"Will you take the job?"

"Oh! Yes, of course! This is a marvellous opportunity! I'm overwhelmed!"

"Well, cease being overwhelmed as soon as you can. You'll need a clear head for this job. Now go and see Miss Halliday and see what assistance she will require."

The next morning I sidled up to Gavin's work-station. "Gavin," I said, "I understand I must congratulate you. You've just been given an extremely prestigious assignment."

"Yes, that's quite right. But how did you know? I thought only Miss Halliday and the Chairman himself..."

I tapped my nose and gave a little smirk.

"Aha!" I interrupted. "There aren't many things the Chairman does that are a secret from me." (I tried to convey the impression that it was I who had suggested Gavin's appointment).

"One of my responsibilities," I went on, "is overall responsibility for the processing of all of EGCol's information services - networking, storage, manipulation and so on. King of the bits, as you might say."

"I didn't know that."

"Don't worry, I'm sure you'll catch on fast. Now, it's particularly important to us senior people in headquarters to know what happens in Rome. I will need accurate accounts of which theatres and opera houses you perform in, the occupancy of seats, each day's takings, the critical reception of individual works - that sort of thing. We need all this information at Board level so we can take informed decisions about the make-up of programmes for future international ventures. Do you understand?"

"I think so..."

"Good. Now, you must remember your prime duty is to remove all day-to-day worries from Miss Halliday's lovely shoulders so that she can concentrate on her choreography and dancing. There's no need - to be blunt, it's highly undesirable - to let Miss Halliday know that we're making these routine reports. But I would be grateful for notes on how she spends her day - time at rehearsals, time on stage, time seeing local dignitaries, that sort of thing. Don't misunderstand me, I don't want you to spy on her - just a few jottings based on your normal observations. After all she is the king-pin of the whole operation, so her health and morale are as important to us as they would be of an astronaut on an important space mission."

"I understand."

"Good. Now, as to mechanics. I have perfected the design of a portable satellite terminal to look like an umbrella and a suit case. You can carry it around with you without arousing curiosity and then, when you're alone - perhaps on the balcony of your hotel room - you can open it and point it to the sky. You move it around until it picks up a satellite homing signal whereupon a gadget looking like a hand calculator will give a read-out as to which satellite you're pointing at and whether there's space capacity. Then you plug in the microphone unit, which is in the umbrella handle..."

"Excuse me for butting in, sir, but if I may say so, carrying umbrellas and briefcases around in Rome in summer is not what you would normally associate with a ballet company, even an English one. Why don't I just use the phone?"

Indeed, why not just use the phone? Brilliant! For a moment I felt a twinge of humiliation at not thinking of the idea myself, but such is my generosity of spirit, I openly acknowledged my appreciation of a penetrating mind. The lad will go far!

CHAPTER THIRTEEN

Grace spent the next few weeks at the Gwendoline Theatre in an unceasing welter of activity. She videophoned almost every well-known choreographer, character dancer and soloist in Europe, enjoying their demonstrations of the steps, leaps and turns of the classical ballet; and watching with attention but distaste the slithers and writhings of its twentieth century successors. She marvelled at the steroid-aided jumps and acrobatic antics of modern dance and snatched at ideas - sometimes little more than a few movements, an angle of head and arm, an arched instep - generated by her fellow choreographers. Composers of every nation and musical persuasion and artists working in every known medium could be found in the theatre's anterooms. In this way - often by virtuoso use of electronic communications in which the dancers, musicians and designers never actually met until the dress rehearsal - Grace, in an astonishing explosion of creativity, produced four new major ballets simultaneously as well as radically revising 'The Seven Deadly Sins'.

As the days went by, dancers, musicians and dress-makers arrived in dribs and drabs to sign contracts with Gavin Wain and join rehearsals of works with which they had already developed an opto-electronic familiarity. The acceleration of financial commitment during those weeks would have been truly frightening had we not had the assurance of Josef Fleck's financial backing.

Grace's four new ballets were: 'Les Nuages'; 'The Temptation of Saint Antonia'; 'Genesis'; and a light-hearted confection, 'Bangers and Mash'. In 'Les Nuages' groups of dancers, to the slithering accompaniment of a battery of musical saws, wafted about the stage to represent various types of cloud formations; for the first fifteen minutes or so this offered mildly pleasant visual images but little dramatic stimulation; then, (presaged by the introduction of timpani into the aural environment), storm clouds burst in, driving the fluffy white cumuli away in terror. The vivid Peruvian dancer, Antonio

Perez, was particularly striking in his depiction of forked lightening in this number.

'The Temptation of Saint Antonia' was set in a harshly-lit bleak rocky landscape, suggestive of the surface of a dead moon. Clouds of fine dust are whipped up as a space capsule descends and lands at one side of the stage; a door slides open, a ladder descends and out steps a dainty female clad in a skin-tight aluminium space suit and a transparent globular helmet. In a dance cleverly composed to suggest a multi-fold reduction in gravity St. Antonia - for it is she - floats and skims between the boulders and over the craters to bring blessings to this barren world and to claim it for the true religion. Very gradually we realise she is not alone: the landscape is not deserted. Creatures of fantastic appearance, some of ethereal beauty, others of repellent ugliness, emerge from behind the rocks and rear up through the granular surface. Antonia's first reaction is to recoil from the Uglies and fall into the arms of the lissome Beauties with whom she willingly dances. Too late does she realise that their embraces are coarsely erotic and that her identification of goodness with beauty does not apply in this alien world. The work concludes with the Uglies driving away the Beauties and clearing a path to her capsule. The curtain descends on the ascension of St. Antonia in a burst of orange flame.

There were several similarities between this ballet and 'The Seven Deadly Sins'; indeed, the music was by the same composer.

'Genesis' was by far the most ambitious of the four new works and was the only one set to a piece of established music - Haydn's 'Creation'. Grace had set herself the difficult task of staging the first chapter of The Bible from a virulently feminist viewpoint. She immediately faced a formidable challenge in her depiction of God: God as an old man with long white hair and flowing beard, swathed in swirling drapes, has been readily acceptable as a creature of infinite dignity and authority for many centuries; it is not nearly so easy to evoke the same gravitas in the person of an old woman. Grace attempted to overcome this problem - to my mind with but qualified success - by giving her female God an immense bouffant mane of silver hair which flowed like wings behind her. God appears from swirling clouds creating light and the firmament and a green steaming Earth; Eve is fashioned from the primeval clay and Adam is formed the next day as a sort of penile adjunct; and it was, of course, Adam who succumbed to the blandishments of the serpent and thereby to eviction from the Garden of Eden. There was an amusing interlude later in the ballet when Noah becomes so roaring drunk (a weakness, apparently, known only to males) that the construction of the Ark is undertaken by his wife and daughters-in-law without his realising his relegation from the role of master craftsman. A charming sequence follows in which the females of all the species - mares, ewes, does, sows, bitches, etc., confidently lead their puzzled and frightened male consorts into the craft. Although I had several reservations about this work, I must admit that the fusion between the sophisticated and the naive, like a collaboration between Piero della Francesca and Le Douanier Rousseau, imparted a vision of striking novelty.

'Bangers and Mash' had no story-line at all. It was a series of divertissements created to demonstrate the virtuosity of this unparalleled company of star dancers, performed against a demonic sound - wall of syncopated percussion.

As well as these four brand-new ballets and a drastically-revised version of 'Sins', Grace revived her favourite early-nineteenth century classics 'La Sylphide' and 'Giselle'. She refrained from including the later romantic Tchaikovsky/Petipa/Ivanov blockbusters because, firstly, their length was far beyond the attention span of contemporary audiences; secondly their inclusion of flashy displays such as entrechats dix and multitudinous fouettés aroused applause amongst the less well-bred members of the audience in mid-scene, thus ruining the atmosphere; and, thirdly, she found the role of the prima ballerina (which, naturally, she, and she alone, would have to undertake) too exhausting. She did make one concession to vulgar exhibitionism, however, in that she allowed her supporting choreographers to revive the old Diaghilev war-horse 'Polovstian Dances': this gave the male members of the company an opportunity to leap about twanging their bows and arrows and displaying their virility.

Hector was a constant visitor to the Gwendoline Theatre during this hectic period. Indeed, he was scarcely ever to be found in his office, a deficiency which led to murmurings from his Board of Directors about neglect of duty, particularly from Lance, who was his reluctant deputy during these absences. There was no doubt in the minds of those of us who were around at that time that Hector was besotted with Grace. He never spoke to her (perhaps because of her polite but positive rejection of his attentions when she first visited Boskey) but his eyes scarcely ever left her elegant person. He would sit in the rehearsal area at the end remote from the barre and mirrors in a great leather chair especially brought across from his office. With chin cupped in hands and elbows on knees, he would stare intently at that lithe wispy figure. Messengers would come from EGCol seeking his voiceprint to agreements or requests for decisions; he would grudgingly give a surly response and then resume his undivided devotion to the flickering silver flame that was Grace Halliday.

Undercurrent rumours and office chit-chat soon reached Gwendoline's ears. She made an unannounced and explosive visit to her theatre to find her husband - just as it had been whispered to her - tucked into his great chair and utterly absorbed in Grace's creation of her solo dance in 'St. Antonia'. Gwendoline plumped herself down beside Hector and uttered a few pithy observations in his ear. His replies were slow, unemotional and inconsequential. She could see he was in another world, a world in which she had no presence.

Lance was equally dismayed by his Chairman's obsession. He was angry because he had been refused the position of business manager to the touring company; he was angry because his Chairman's dereliction of duty had thrown additional burdens upon him as Managing Director; and he was deeply upset because Grace was, after all, his niece and he felt that in his position as locus parentis he should actively discourage the attentions of an older married man.

It did not need my intellect to be working at full throttle to foresee that unless Hector pulled himself out of his emotional morass a crisis would develop which would gravely affect our entire company. It was no good talking to him direct: he was deaf to all comments of a personal nature. I could think of only one person who might influence him positively: his mother, Lady Iris. As I made my way to her cottage, glowing rosily in the dusk, I wondered how the passing years would have affected The Grand Old Dame of Boskey. I need not have worried: there was grey in her hair and lines by her mouth but she was as upright in posture and as sharp in mind as ever.

I described the situation diffidently, haltingly: it is not easy to tell a mother that her only beloved son has gone off the rails. She heard me out in grave attention. Then she said "Thank you for telling me. I will see what I can do."

Next day it was common knowledge throughout the EGCol offices that Hector had been summoned to attend upon his mother that evening. (Gwendoline didn't accompany him... it was one of her drama evenings... she said she was playing the lead in Wedekind's 'Lulu'). Hector arrived promptly but sullenly and received a withering dressing-down from his mother He heard it out in silence. Then he replied:

"Mother, I have always valued the advice and guidance you have given me in the past. I know more than anyone how EGCol's success has depended upon your wisdom. But that was back in the days when I was an inexperienced youth. I have now been Chairman of a prosperous - and increasingly prospering - company for more than a decade and I know what I'm doing. I am well aware that there has been criticism of the time I have spent during the last few weeks watching Grace Halliday at work. But, in case you are unaware of the facts of the case, mother, let me tell you that Miss Halliday is on my Board of Directors, that she has been entrusted with a most important mission that has enormous potential for our company and that I must take it upon myself to be convinced that the preparations she is making for this venture are correct in every detail." He then strode - no, that's too dramatic a term for poor weedy Hector - he shuffled out of his mother's home.

But that was not the end of the day's drama: it peaked when he arrived back at Dromdeal Tower to be informed by his petrified staff that Gwendoline had eloped with Lance.

CHAPTER FOURTEEN

For someone so seemingly unworldly, Grace Halliday showed a remarkable grasp of the importance of publicity. She persuaded Hector, without much difficulty, that the entire company should travel on its world tours in a special train of cable cars painted in ruby red with 'Princess Ruby Royal Ballet Company' picked out along its length in white and gold. Gavin Wain didn't have the pleasure of seeing this noble vehicle in its pristine state; he had travelled in advance of the party to Rome and had videophoned back to say that he had hired the Colosseum, no less, for the first part of the tour. Moreover, he had secured enough accommodation in some of Rome's most splendid and central hotels for every member of the company, with a particularly prestigious suite looking out over the restored Forum for Grace. The expense was horrendous but no-one was worrying.

Apart from a reserve staff in the EGCol offices to keep watch on incoming messages, the whole of Boskey turned out to see the company take off from Charlie's Fields. It was certainly a diverting sight, with the dancers prancing and mincing their way to the leading carriage and the more sober musicians following behind placing their instruments with exaggerated care into the baggage car. Finally, to the huzzahs of the multitude, Grace herself appeared, dressed entirely in white relieved by a belt of silver links around her tiny waist and long silver braid ribbons flowing from her wimple. As she tripped daintily to the first car, all eyes in the Fields turned to Hector, sitting alone in the Chairman's great double seat; they were expecting signs of emotion, but he, twisted in his usual hunched posture, displayed nothing. The crowd, disappointed at this lack of human drama, turned back to cheer as the great train slowly left the Fields and trundled towards the junction with the trunk route to the coast whence it would speed over the Channel to France, the Alps and Italy.

Gavin phoned me the next day to report that the company had arrived without incident, had settled into their hotels and that rehearsals had already commenced. He was delighted at having booked the Colosseum for their debut; it had been fully restored to operational use in the early years of this century and was certainly one of the most spectacular performance venues in the world. Its peculiar shape and grandiose nature, however, had necessitated drastic revisions to the staging of some of the ballets, most of which had been designed with a proscenium arch in mind. It was no longer possible, for instance, for the capsule in 'St. Antonia' to descend on to stage as though from outer space. But, making a virtue out of necessity, (in an idea which Gavin modestly attributed to himself), the spacecraft was dangled from an immense mobile crane which, in full view of the audience, crisscrossed by coherent laser beams, emerged slowly out of the darkness and deposited the capsule upon the stage for Grace to make her sensational entrance. In their original format, the knockabout frivolities of 'Bangers and Mash' seemed tiny and insubstantial in this immense arena, but acquired hilarious impact by being repeated on a multitude of huge video walls. 'Genesis' benefited enormously from the circular stage and the cerulean sky. (Rome's notorious smog had virtually disappeared since the abolition of automobiles).

I reported this promising start to Hector, who had moved back to his EGCol office. He received the news apathetically; clearly his mind was on other things.

Mark Cornwall had been replaced as Director of Marketing by Lionel Madder, a pleasant enough young man who had much of Mark's imagination but none, fortunately, of his ostentatious ambition. Lionel greatly admired Hector and was distressed to see him so listless. He convened an informal meeting of the directors.

"We can't let Hector go on like this." he said. "I'm aware that our current portfolio of products should keep the company ticking over for some time, but that's only if we retain the market's confidence. If the word gets out that we have a demoralised chairman we will lose the support of our financial backers and our major customers."

"I agree," said Kendall, "but what can we do about it?"

"We've got to present him with an idea so attractive," said Wain, "that he will snap out of his black dog mood and become actively involved".

"Sounds all right in theory," said Perceval. "Have you got any ideas?"

"Not yet," admitted Madder, "but I'm thinking hard."

"You'd better be smart," said Perceval. "The Board meeting's next Monday."

"I'll try to present something special," said Madder. "You'll back me up won't you?"

In spite of Lionel Madder's presence the following Monday, the Board of Directors meeting seemed miserably under strength. Grace Halliday was absent, of course, in her march on Rome; and Lance... well, the scandalous loss of his bulky figure left a substantial vacancy at the Chairman's side. Hector squirmed in his chair, bit his lips and glowered at his directors. "Let's get on with it," he said.

So, the Board went through its usual routine, reporting on the progress of current projects, analysing the financials, reviewing the staff position, approving the latest batch of press releases and PR videos, until it came to the penultimate item on the agenda : 'Possible New Projects'. This was Lionel's big moment.

"With your permission, Chairman," he began, "I would like to offer a short presentation on a product that will be of inestimable benefit to the community and highly profitable to EGCol."

Hector raised an eyebrow, thrust his chin even further into his chest, and said nothing.

"As we know only too well," Lionel went on, "the human constitution is subject to an immense variety of illnesses, weaknesses, distempers and strains. Some of these are caused by physical impacts, some by external agencies such as viruses and contagious diseases; but a large number are the cumulative effect of activities within our own control, such as drug-taking, over-eating, over-drinking, over-stimulation of almost any of our senses, smoking, solvent snif fing, bastinado, simulated strangulation..."

"I get the picture," snapped Hector. "Get on with it."

"All these activities," continued Lionel, "pleasurable though they may be, have a deleterious effect on our organs and, when taken to excess, result in malfunctions, illness... even death. But how much is too much? What does 'taken to excess' mean? How can we avoid taking our self-indulgencies beyond the limit when serious health problems occur? But, on the other hand, why should we call a halt to these simple pleasures when there may still be a substantial safety margin in hand?

"The designers of inanimate systems - trains, planes, automobiles, telecommunications, television studios - have tackled similar problems over the years and have arrived at a variety of solutions ranging from the simple to the sophisticated. Take the, now largely obsolete, automobile. When it was running low on fuel, an audible signal would sound to attract the driver's attention and a line drawing of a petrol pump would appear in a small visual display; or, if low in lubricant, an oil-can; or, if lacking coolant, a thermometer... and so on and so on. To take a more complex example, a telephone system consists largely of opto-electronic switching units interconnected by transmission links; should any item fail, a standby unit is automatically switched into place and the code number and location of the faulty item is signalled back to central maintenance control from where remedial action can be instigated.

"We are not likely during our generation to reach the happy stage when a standby organ is automatically switched into place if one of them malfunctions; but we might in the nearer term emulate the automobile and the other systems I mentioned by having supervisory and alarm signals which warn us of incipient internal problems before real harm is done. You may say we have such a built-in indicator already - pain. But pain, besides being unpleasant, usually comes too late: by the time we experience pain our kidneys or liver or heart or whatever the problem areas might be are already in deep trouble. I suggest, Chairman, that what mankind needs is a pain-free indicator which warns us that if we continue with our favourite self-abuse without let-up then such-and-such an organ will fail; we can then phase out that particular indulgence over the next few weeks and so avoid irreparable damage. We then, perhaps, seek our pleasures elsewhere.

"I am happy to say that electromagnetomedical technology has now reached a stage of development when such a system is within our grasp. The first manifestation would be a slim pad, one side studded with sensors, which would be strapped to the inside of the left forearm. The sensors would monitor blood pressure, pulse, blood viscosity, skin resistance, synaptic transmission times and a dozen other key parameters. It would, I believe, be embarrassing to have a visual or aural read-out of the deductions made by the integrated microprocessor - other people might be around in ear- or eye-shot - so I suggest the unit should be detached from the arm before bed-time and jacked into the home display unit. We then see - hopefully - messages such as LIVER OK LUNGS OK HEART OK, etc - or, as a cause of concern - LIVER SYMPTOMS SLIGHTLY ABNORMAL CUT DOWN ON BRANDY. It is a device such as this, Chairman, that I propose we should construct in an experimental model form. I imagine that future versions will be sufficiently miniaturised to be implanted beneath the forearm skin, but that is beyond our current capabilities."

Lionel sat down and looked expectantly at Hector. If he was hoping for words of congratulation, he was disappointed. Hector sat hunched in introspection and said not a word. The silence became oppressive. Keith Kendall, unbidden, offered his contribution.

"As I'm sure you are aware, Chairman, it's difficult to prepare a definitive business plan for a revolutionary concept. There are no existing data on the size of the market, the rate of take-up, the price consumers are prepared to pay and all the other variables we need to construct a spread-sheet.

"Nevertheless, we have had a preliminary look at Lionel's proposals and believe that if we have a clear run of a year before competitors enter the field this could be one of the most profitable projects that EGCol has even launched."

Another dead silence. Hector squirmed in his chair, bit his fingers but said nothing. Perceval broke the tension.

"I expect you are wondering, Chairman, whether this project is technically feasible. Well, my lads have put Lionel's concept on the operating table, so to speak, and taken it apart, and although there may be some medical conditions which we can't identify in our first models - the presence of gall-stones, for example - we are confident that most of the sensing and interpreting techniques are within the state of the art. Admittedly, we would need expert medical advice on what were the acceptable/unacceptable boundaries for each organ's function; what we have in mind is to approach several different hospitals and universities so that no one organisation is able to construct the complete picture of our mission from our individual collaborative ventures."

Hector groaned but said nothing. The other directors looked at me to see whether I could fan some life into the discussion. I wondered whether I could arouse Hector from his torpor by playing devil's advocate.

"This is all very well, gentlemen," I said, sweeping the great oval table with a mock censuring look, "but what about the ethical aspects of this proposal?"

"Ethical! Ethical!" stuttered Lionel Madder "Of course it's ethical! It saves people from pain and unnecessarily damaging their bodies!"

"Ah, yes!" I said. "That's my point. By letting people know how far they can go without irreversible damage, you are encouraging them to indulge in a vice up to a prescribed limit; having reached it they switch to another one and then to another. It will turn us into a society of smoke-filled drunken hop-heads who are not quite dead but ought to be."

The Board appeared not to appreciate my attempt to stir up an intellectual discussion. Perceval summed up the general feeling: "Oh, do shut up, you daft old bugger!" he said.

This acrimonious exchange did at least have the effect of arousing Hector. He rubbed his eyes, straightened himself in his chair, and swept the table in a steady glance. We fell silent, awaiting his verdict: were we to proceed with the experimental phase or did he want more studies before he allocated funds?

"I'll get those bastards!" he spluttered. "I'll get them!"

CHAPTER FIFTEEN

Young Gavin phoned me daily from Rome with news about the company's reception. 'St. Antonia', 'Genesis', and 'Seven Deadly Sins' had been highly successful and had received resounding applause on the first few nights of the season. 'Nuages' didn't seem to arouse much emotion, positive or negative, but was left as the opening item of the programme whilst the patrons were noisily finding their places. The Italians didn't see anything funny in 'Bangers and Mash'; they either tried to disinter some dark hidden symbolism (the critics) or pelted it with oranges (the public). Those splendid old classics 'La Sylphide' and 'Giselle' were actively disliked and were replaced in the programme after the first week by extra performances of 'Seven Deadly Sins' - much more to red-blooded Latin taste. On the whole there had been sympathetic reviews on most of the cable arts channels and attendances at the Colosseum, after a slow start, were very encouraging - usually well above 80% capacity. So reported young Gavin.

Good, fine, splendid, I responded. But what of Miss Grace? Was she standing up to the pressure? Was the double burden of being prima ballerina and artistic director too much for her? Not at all, said Gavin, she seems to be revelling in her stardom. She was constantly in demand for interviews and her ethereal face graced every video magazine. Her huge hotel apartment was never-endingly a-blossom with bouquets from countless admirers.

And did she have many visitors? I inquired. Yes, VIPs of all sorts - politicians, religious dignitaries, chief executives of the armed forces... as well as lesser fry, such as journalists and ballet-lovers. Any scientists? I asked. Not yet, said Gavin, somewhat surprised. Why, was I expecting any? Who knows? I replied offhandedly.

Hector was pleased to learn that his emissary was the toast of Rome, but most of his attention and energy was directed towards the ruination of Lance and Gwendoline. Lance's return to the North had been warmly welcomed by the Hadrian Group. Up to then, the Group had been a loose association of comparatively small companies but now they had the opportunity of being brought together into one cohesive force under a Group Managing Director - Lance - possessing an intimate knowledge of their principal competitor's plans and strategies. Hector decided to move before Lance had time to co-ordinate his units: he had a list drawn up of all the products that EGCol and the Hadrian Group had in common and promptly instigated a savage price war. Keith Kendall, the Director of Finance, was alarmed.

"I hope you know what you're doing, guv'nor," he said. "If you're trying to drive our competitors out of business I must, with respect, warn you that your tactics could be counter-productive. Some of our products are now being sold at less than cost price. We can't go on for long like this without having to call upon our reserves."

"It's a question of nerve,' responded Hector. "They will crack before I do."

"I do hope so," said Kendall. "I really do hope so."

Although Hector no longer confided in or consulted his mother, I knew in my bones that Lady Iris would not remain inactive in this time of crisis, so I started monitoring her home every day. One evening I heard her setting up a meeting, to be held in two day's time, with her three half-sisters, Elaine, Morwaine and Fay The thought of Fay being in the neighbourhood jellified my limbs and brain; I had to lay my head on the table for a few minutes before I regained control. Even then I could think of little else but: I must see her! I must see her!

On the day of the meeting I disguised myself as an artist painting the row of cottages of which Lady Iris's was the roseate glory. Dressed in a long cloak and crowned by a floppy beret, I sat on the other side of the High Street daubing at a canvas with more zeal than skill. (I received some uncomplimentary remarks from passers-by who didn't readily accept my explanation that I was in the avant-garde of a totally new school of visual expression). The shadows were growing long and my buttocks had become paralysed by the framework of my folding stool when Elaine and Morwaine arrived; without a glance in my direction they were admitted into Lady Iris's cottage. A few moments later, Fay arrived, dressed in stately black and gold. She stood at the door of the cottage and then, slowly, coolly and deliberately, she turned and, looking fully at me, unleashed a devastating icy smile. My organs dissolved into a wrenching plasma. She had felt my presence! She had acknowledge my existence! It took an immense concentration of will to gather up my artistic impedimenta and scuttle back to my own home in order to activate my electronic tap into Lady Iris's drawing room.

The four ladies sat in a still grave circle. Although their conversation touched some emotional issues, this was scarcely ever reflected in raised voices or unseemly expressions. Lady Iris explained the situation succinctly then concluded by saying:

"So, I trust you will share my concern. I expect that you, like me, are greatly distressed to see someone behaving irresponsibly in such an important position as Hector's and I'm sure you will appreciate that, as the most prominent figure in Boskey society, any opprobrium he attracts will reflect on Boskey as a whole. Inevitably our great artistic community will founder Further, we are all major shareholders in EGCol and if that company is driven into insolvency we shall all be severely affected financially. And, finally - and this is a worry that must affect me personally far more than it does you - Hector is my son, and in spite of his moods and occasional follies, I love him dearly."

"You're not alone in that," said Morwaine. "I'm sure we all have the deepest affection for him. But if you're worried about the chairmanship of EGCol whilst his mind is - I'm sure, temporarily - disturbed, then dismiss that worry from your mind. There's always my son to take over if need be."

"And mine," said Elaine.

"Yours!" said Morwaine. "He's still in his teens!"

"But he's very advanced for his years," said Elaine. "Remember who his father is."

"That was not an episode to be proud of," observed Fay. "I would keep quiet about it if I were you."

"Ladies! Ladies!" intervened Lady Iris. "What is all this talk about who becomes chairman? We are a long, long way from even considering deposing Hector He has an imaginative genius and a business acumen second to none. It's just that he has been unsettled by a succession of emotional crises. I was hoping that together we could devise a way to bring him back to sanity."

Morwaine and Elaine sat back in their chairs and folded their arms. Fay turned towards Lady Iris; on her smooth marble countenance there was an expression of ageless wisdom, such as one occasionally sees on the faces of old dogs and chimpanzees.

"We can best bring him back to normal," she said, " by accepting that he is obsessed by the thought of ruining the Hadrian Group and humiliating Lance and Gwendoline. If we can help him to accomplish this as soon as possible he will bring this devastating war to an end. He can then re-direct his talents to driving EGCol to even greater heights; he'll be able to sponsor further artistic projects and bring world renown to Boskey Common.:

"Yes, I see, yes," said Lady Iris reflectively. "And how can he accelerate the overthrow of the Hadrians?"

"By doing to them what they attempted to do to him so many years ago. He should travel in person with some of his senior directors right into the enemy's territory and set up a staff interview centre. He can then offer salaries and packages of benefits to their personnel that are so attractive that half of their staff will be scrambling to join him here in the South. The combination of price-cutting and staff disaffection should be enough to ruin the Group. He can then travel home in triumph, perhaps bringing a few prize specimens with him, leaving Lance as the Group Managing Director of a group of companies that have become little more than shells; and with Gwendoline as the poule de luxe of someone who can't provide luxe any more."

"Do you think Gwendoline will go back to Hector?" asked

Morwaine.

"It's more question as to whether he wants her back," observed Elaine tartly. "If he really is as besotted as we have heard with this skinny little toe-dancer then Gwendoline will have no home to come back to."

Lady Iris was distressed to hear this casual reference to her son's infidelity and turned the discussion back to Fay's proposal.

"I really think you have the basis of a workable strategy there, Fay. Would anyone like a glass of New Mexican port whilst we ponder?"

She moved to the sideboard and poured some deep brown fluid into small crystal glasses. Whilst her back was turned Fay grasped her two sisters by the hand and transmitted them a wink that would have skewered a passing butterfly. Her smile of complicity turned swiftly back to a mien of thoughtful composure as Lady Iris came back with the drinks.

I had, of course, been watching all this on my monitor. This rapid display of gestures and expressions shocked me into the realisation that Fay and the others were deceiving their hostess. Fay was being false to her own half-sister. Could my mind accept that revelation? Fay was false!

Gavin's phone call the following morning dwelt too long, I felt, on the box-office takings at the Colosseum and the ebbing and flowing of the fickle Roman public's likes and dislikes. The management of the giant amphitheatre had just installed public reaction control knobs at the side of every seat. At the end of each work the viewers would adjust their controls to show their appreciation level at so many points out of ten. If more than 50% of the audience registered four or less, a huge downward-pointing thumb would appear on a giant screen at the end of the stadium; if six or more it would point upwards; in between... a dithering horizontal. Italian composers and choreographers had been known to throw themselves into the Tiber if they ever received the thumbs-down; but Grace's phlegmatic Brits weren't upset so easily and would merely mutter archaic proverbs such as "Ah, well, back to the drawing board" when an inverted 10-metre thumb glowed in derision.

According to Gavin, Grace continued to be the focus of Roman society; she now received so many visitors she was adopting a Canova-like posture upon a chaise-longue and lifted a languid hand to receive the kisses of her admirers. This had proved a little embarrassing, said Gavin, when one of her visitors entered her suite in a wheel-chair and found himself nose-to-nose with the fair enchantress. Wheelchair! I interrupted, wheel-chair! (trying not to sound too excited), who was it in the wheel-chair? It was a distinguished American scientist, who ran an advanced chemical research centre in Vatican City. Was it a long conversation? I asked. I couldn't tell you, said Gavin, you told me not to spy on her. Of course, of course, I said. But there is one thing I can tell you, Gavin went on, Miss Halliday must have made an impression on him because he has offered to take her on a tour of his laboratories next Sunday when there are no company performances and the research centre is quiet.

Marvellous! Everything was going to plan!

I had just concluded this conversation when I saw from my entrance hall monitor that Lady Iris had entered the EGCol building. This was most unusual: I doubt whether she had been there since the occasion, all those years ago, when she had brought young Hector along with his communications module. She created a sensation in the foyer: receptionists and security guards were tumbling over one another to attend to her. She maintained her lofty composure until someone had the sense to take her to Hector's office. Fifteen minutes later, Kendall and Perceval were summoned to the sanctum.

"Lady Pennington has just suggested a plan" said Hector, "which I believe has a great deal of merit. In outline, it is that we three should move into the Hadrian Group's own territory and set up a recruiting centre - just as they did to me when I first took over EGCol. We will offer their best people terms and conditions which they can scarcely refuse and, at the same time, step up the price war. With the market share swinging our way and with wholesale staff resignations, the Group will suffer a drastic loss of confidence and share prices will plunge. When they've reached their nadir we will step in and buy as many shares as we can before the City analysts wake up. We'll then... er... rationalise the product range of the two groups."

"Hold on," protested Kendall. "We can't take on all those people you will have recruited. We don't have the vacancies - and, what's more, with your price-cutting campaign in full swing, we don't have the cash-flow to pay them."

"I said we would offer them positions," said Hector. "I didn't say we would actually take them on."

"But... " uttered Kendall and Perceval, utterly shocked, in unison, "That's unethical!"

"There are times when the ends justify the means," Hector pronounced ponderously.

"Where have I heard that before?" muttered Perceval.

"Eh? What?" snarled Hector. "No more discussion. Tomorrow we go to Vindolanda."

CHAPTER SIXTEEN

I swiftly contacted our provincial office closest to the midpoint of Hadrian's wall to warn them that their Chairman and two senior directors would shortly be wanting of fice and domestic accommodation near Vindolanda. The news caused a flurry; our colleagues out in the sticks were not accustomed to dealing with such high-powered dignitaries and worried themselves into a lather as to how they should comport themselves. I tried to calm their jitters: just call Hector 'Chairman' when addressing him, I said, and provide whatever he requires as soon as humanly possible without argument. This advice, kindly meant, didn't seem to reduce the tension very much.

The departure of Hector and his two lieutenants to the North and of the three beautiful, but wicked, sisters to their homes, left me little of interest to monitor in the EGCol offices or in Boskey Common in general. I turned back to Josef Teck's yacht, the 'QMIII', which had escaped my attention for some time. The crew and staff were in a far more agitated state than when I had last electronically dropped in on them. The signals I was picking up on my paraboloid resembled a wasps' nest being stirred with a thick stick. But Teck's voice boomed through all the chaotic babble - tetchy, argumentative, abusive, browbeating. As far as I could make out he was buying and selling shares in companies, and sometimes whole companies or even groups of companies, with bewildering speed. There were occasions when he sold, bought back, then sold again the same company on the same day. So this is how a great financial mogul operates, I thought: Teck is obviously on the point of accomplishing a great financial coup and in a few days' time he will be able to buy another Sargent for his stateroom and a Bulgarian beauty for his bedroom. Should I buy some Teck stock and make my own modest pile?

At one point these high-speed high-powered machinations were interrupted by a more domestic matter of particular interest to me. From what I could gather from Teck's roars and barks at his staff, The

Princess Ruby Ballet had forwarded him a bundle of invoices from the Colosseum, several hotels and innumerable restaurants. Teck ordered an assistant to make up a complete list of all those bodies having the impertinence to request payment and sent them all the identical hologram:

"I confirm I am underwriting all expenses incurred by the Princess Ruby Royal Ballet. Your demands will be met in full in due course. Meanwhile don't bother me by repeating or augmenting applications for payment whilst I am engaged in important and complex business negotiations. Teck."

I sought out the young man who had temporarily taken over the Finance Department whilst Keith Kendall was accompanying Hector and told him about the frenetic burst of energy in Teck's headquarters.

"Don't take too much notice," he advised. "These great entrepreneurs are often like that. They'll spend weeks playing golf or whale-watching and they come back to base with a fistful of new ideas to try out."

"Yes, I can understand that," I said, " but could I profit from my inside knowledge by investing a little of my savings into some Teck companies?"

The young man looked at me severely. "I understand you have been advising EGCol for a long time," he said.

"Yes, back to the days when our present Chairman's grandfather was running the company."

"So you must know - in fact, you probably wrote it - that one of the tenets of our company is to deal in ethical products and services only."

"Yes, but... "

"What do you think of Teck's way of doing business? Strictly ethical?"

"Well, no, but I wasn't thinking of involving EGCol. This would be a purely private deal."

"So, you make a distinction, do you, between what you advise the company to do and what you are prepared to do yourself?"

He withered me with a stare.

"No, no, of course not," I muttered.

Pompous young prig.

The Princess Ruby Royal Ballet season in Rome was coming to its end. The company, so said young Gavin, was sizzling with joie-de-vivre, so great had been its acclaim. The last appearance was on the Thursday evening of the third week of the visit when all the works that had become favourites with the Roman audiences were performed: it started with a rip-roaring rendition of 'Polovstian Dances', followed by 'Seven Deadly Sins', 'Genesis' and 'St.Antonia'. The last three works all starred Grace who, far from being exhausted, appeared centre stage at the end of the last ballet as fresh as mother's milk. The vast platform became the bedrock of a hillock of flowers and the cheers of the audience could be heard on all seven hills.

Gavin was late in calling me the following morning - he had indulged a little too deeply in the celebratory party - and told me that Grace, in appreciation of all their hard work, had granted the entire company a five-day holiday to stay on in their hotels and do whatever they pleased. She recommended they should visit the art galleries and marvel at the many splendid buildings but added, with a twinkle, that she wouldn't think any the worse of them if they sampled the shops, the food, the wine or whatever gave them joy. She, however, was returning immediately to England because she needed to report urgently to the Chairman of EGCol. I leaned forward and stared at my videophone.

"Do you know what this report is about?" I asked.

"Not really," he said. "But I do know that when she returned from her visit to the American research place last Sunday she was carrying a shiny metal suitcase. I have a feeling it's something to do with that."

So Grace, sweet Grace, amazing Grace, had been successful. She had radiated purity and dependability and Dr. Fischer had trusted her with a specimen of GRAIL to bring back to EGCol. She was expected back in Boskey Common the following day. That's a pity, I thought. I can imagine her rushing along to the EGCol office with her shiny metal case, brimming over with her account of the last three weeks, only to discover that Hector and the other Board members had sallied North. Never mind, it would keep, it would keep.

Meanwhile Hector and his colleagues had had a very satisfactory few days. They had rented a suite of rooms in an inn, the 'Ada Augusta', and were receiving a steady stream of Hadrian Group personnel who had learned from the local cable news that EGCol was recruiting on a massive scale and offering unparalled inducements to join the company. Hadrian's directors had no difficulty in deducing that although Hector's attack on them could be expected in the normal run of business, it was the presence of Lance, his erstwhile friend and lieutenant, as their Group Managing Director, not to mention Lance's abduction of Gwendoline, that had added especial venom to the onslaught. Lance was suddenly recognised as being more of a burden that a benefit and was ordered to clear his desk forthwith after scarcely a month in office.

Meanwhile, back at my information hub, I was monitoring Teck's actions with increasing intensity and concern. I was certainly glad that Keith Kendall's deputy had shamed me out of investing in Teck's companies, because I was beginning to realise that Teck was not about to pull off some amazing coup - which I had at first thought was the reason behind his frenzied activity - but was in deep financial trouble. He was selling far more that he was buying and was frantically transferring funds from company to company and from deposit to deposit, presumably with the intention of confusing anyone trying to uncover the true state of his financial standing. A charity he had set up three years' ago for the benefit of injured African squash players was being unmercifully raided. I suddenly recalled the Ruby Ballet's request for payment of countless expenses incurred in Rome and Teck's curt reply. Grace herself had escaped but what of the rest of the company?

Hector wouldn't leave his interviewing to answer my call to the 'Ada Augusta' so I sent a videogram. It ran:-

"I have reason to believe Teck is suffering financial problems. Our ballet company in Rome is dependent on his meeting all accommodation, travel and general sponsorship bills which he has so far refused to honour. Grace is on her way back home but the rest of the company is 'on holiday' happily believing all expenses will be paid. I earnestly request you to contact Teck immediately to ensure he gives priority to allocating whatever is left of his resources to our people in Rome.

Regards Melvyn".

A few hours later I received a reply:-

"You can't expect me to confront Teck on such a sensitive matter on the basis of unsubstantiated rumours. Our relationship is highly dependent on mutual trust. In any case my Closed User Group access to share prices gives no reason for concern. If ballet company personnel have difficulty in meeting bills I authorise you to sort out the problem with assistance of EGCol Finance Division.

Pennington."

I knew without having to consult the finance division that EGCol did not have the liquidity to meet the cost of the Rome venture.

The next burst of news about Teck didn't come from any of my monitoring systems: it came, for the whole world to see and hear, from the syndicated 24 Hour News Channel. It reported that the world-famous tycoon and philanthropist, Josef Teck, had that morning travelled from his yacht to the international travel station at Albi in Southern France and had boarded a flight to Samoa. About an hour after take-off he had moved into the air-lock area and, in spite of the protestations of the hostess and the physical intervention of the steward, Teck forced them aside, donned a maintenance engineer's space-suit and stepped out of the vehicle. He was now in a low-level elliptical orbit; upon re-entry into the atmosphere he would be burned to a crisp.

(It was not until later we learned that Teck's financial problems were largely due to imprudently heavy investment in the Hadrian Group of companies).

CHAPTER SEVENTEEN

Just as I had expected, Grace was at the EGCol offices at dawn the next day, greatly disappointed at Hector's not being there to receive her. After congratulating her on the success of her Roman foray - at which she blushed prettily - I explained that Hector's current obsession was the ruin and disgrace of Lance and Gwendoline, to which the collapse of the Hadrian Group had all but taken second place. Grace's great blue eyes widened when she heard of Hector's overwhelming hatred for Lance and Gwendoline.

"You don't think I... ?" she queried fearfully."

"Of course not!" I reassured her. "Nothing to do with you at all."

"I have something I must give to Mr Pennington," she said. "What's more, now that Mr Teck has disappeared I must ensure that my troupe are able to return from Rome and that we meet all our expenses. So, it's important I see Mr Pennington immediately."

"I do understand, my dear," I assured her, "really I do. But I must advise you not to interrupt him until he has concluded his recruitment drive. You know how single-minded he gets. I'm sure he'll be able to deal with your problems within the next few days."

"They're not just my problems," she protested. "Think of the huge sums of money we have spent on the Princess Ruby Ballet. I'm safe here back at home but all my friends in the company will be thrown in prison if they can't meet their bills. Could I speak to Mr Kendall instead?"

"He's up North, too."

She slumped in her chair in frustration. I tried to comfort her, but she could envisage nothing but travail ahead of her.

My principal frustration was that I had no means of monitoring the events in Vindolanda or within the Hadrian Group. None of my satellite systems was useful because I had no means of locating the transmitting terminal in the 'Ada Augusta' or in the Hadrian offices; and it was a difficult technical problem to tap unobtrusively the optical fibre lines that had long since replaced copper wires. The best I could do as a start was to locate the hideaway that Lance and Gwendoline had move into following Lance's ignominious dismissal. The country had just moved into the situation whereby telecomms services were provided by one national company (NTC) in competition with some other carriers and about five hundred independent local companies. I guessed that Lance would seek a connection to a small local company first and then transfer to, or be duplicated by, the more reliable and secure NTC when he and Gwendoline had settled into their love-nest. I got one of the lads in our Cumbrian office to contact all the local telecomms companies to see whether a Lance Mere had recently become a subscriber. Within 24 hours I had his number and address. My Cumbrian contact knew the area: it was a small village about 12km from Wallsend, open to the invigorating winds that swept across the moor - in other words, bleak. I imagined a substantial cottage constructed of rough stone slabs, with logs for the open fire piled up in an outside shed; roses were around the door, but they had long since expired from exposure to the northern blasts.

I decided to tease Hector by letting him know some of what I knew but not all of what I knew. I sent him a videogram:-

"Have located abode of Lance and Gwendoline. Grace has returned safely to Boskey Common. Rest of troupe still in Rome. Regards - Melvyn."

With two hours (probably during a lunchbreak in the interviewing programme) came the response:-

"Send precise address. Pennington."

I did.

For the next part of this report I must acknowledge my debt to James Perceval who made these notes on his pocket audio cassette:

'When Hector received Melvyn's message giving Lance's address, he swore and ranted that he would descend upon them and do them a terrible mischief: but he couldn't do it that evening because he was meeting the Board of the Hadrian Group to discuss terms for the termination of the trade war. He therefore commanded me to find the cottage, to spy out whether Lance and Gwendoline were there, to keep an eye on their comings and goings and report back the following day.

'"But, guv'nor," I said, "that would involve staying out all night in cold, wet and inhospitable terrain surrounded by wild dogs, coypu, escaped panthers and poisonous snakes."

'"Take a sleeping bag." he said.

'I travelled by cable car to Wallsend and thence on a single track system to Rydon. The attendant gave me further instructions before swinging off to Prudhoe and Wexham. I trudged the rest of the distance - at least 3km - before I located the cottage, lights ablaze, sheltering in a dale. I crept up and peeped through a window. Lance was there, huddled in a chair before a log fire, head bowed in his hands, a phantom of his former self. Gwendoline was bending over him and although I couldn't hear what she was saying, she was obviously giving him a thorough verbal lambasting. I guessed that the cottage wasn't the palace she was hoping for.

'It seemed unlikely that the unhappy couple would move on anywhere that night so I slunk to the dry-walled edge of their demesne and settled under a tree. I admit that as I wriggled into my sleeping bag I began to think fearfully of all the nocturnal creatures that abide in those far from gentle parts.

'Then a strange thing happened. From out of the darkness a small animal came snuffling towards me. I shivered in morbid anticipation. A miniature wolf? No, when it came nearer I could see it was a Pekingese. It settled down at my feet and turned its squashed snotty little face to the outer darkness. Somehow I felt comforted by its presence and fell sound asleep. When dawn broke I awoke completely refreshed. The little dog rose to its feet, yawned with a sound like helium escaping from a child's balloon and trotted off. It had guarded me through the night.

'I made my way back to the 'Ada Augusta', marked the location of Lance's cottage on a map and told Hector the two renegades were in residence. He had come to the end of his interviews and was anxious to confront Lance without delay. His own private cable car was ready so he, Keith and I were soon speeding along to Wallsend then off on the branch line to Rydon. He blanched at the prospect of a 3km walk; fortunately surface vehicles are still permitted in those parts in view of the limited cable coverage and the scattered locations of the dwellings, so we hired a vintage Long Ranger together with its veteran driver and bounced off to chez Mere. I was wondering what on earth Hector would do when he finally came face-to-face with Lance: it would be unwise to indulge in fisticuffs - Lance was a powerful man and could have eaten Hector for a cocktail snack - and as far as I knew, Hector had no proficiency in any of the weapons used in duelling. I had not reckoned on Lance's downcast state and eviscerated morale.

'We arrived at the cottage door. Hector turned to Keith and me and invited us to kick it down. We looked at each other in apprehension. This was scarcely legal, was it? Shouldn't one knock politely first? Come to that, it wasn't very ethical. Hector didn't have time for debate. "Do it!" he roared. We obediently gave the door a reverberating kick and walked over it into the living room. Lance was still sitting where I had seen him the previous evening in front of the lacy ashes of an extinct wood fire. He briefly lifted his head from his hands at this violent intrusion.

'"Where's Gwendoline?" shouted Hector.

'Lance gave a racking sob.

'"Where's Gwendoline? roared Hector again.

'"She's gone off to an Earth-life commune," choked Lance. "It's on the other side of the lake."

'Hector flung me a furious glance, doubting the accuracy of my report. "She was here last night," I said. "It's true, boss, I saw her."

'"She went off early this morning," said Lance, corroborating my statement.

'"What the hell is an Earth-life commune?" demanded Hector, hopping up and down with vexation.

'"It's a group of about twenty or thirty people," Lance explained wearily. "They claim to have dropped out of modern society - no money, no fine clothes, no mechanical or electrical aids other than the simplest hand tools, no fancy goods, no entertainment. They live in a heap of burnt-out motor cars, railway carriages and plane fuselages at the side of the lake. They eat root vegetables and whatever small animals - rabbits, stoat, mink - they can catch and roast over an open fire."

'"I can't imagine Gwen... Mrs Pennington living under such conditions," said Keith.

'"Neither can I," said Lance bitterly, "but that's where she said she was going.

'Hector had allowed his passion to cool a little whilst learning what had happened to his wife. He started stoking up his fires of wrath again.

'"It's utterly disgraceful that my wife should have left my side," he shouted. "But I have no doubt, no doubt at all, that the fault is all yours. I don't know how you did it - perhaps you drugged or hypnotised her - but I'm certain you dragged her away from me against her will. She has never before now strayed from the path of fidelity and has always, always, reciprocated my love."

'(Kendall and I glanced at one another and restrained a smirk).

'Hector's voice was rising in pitch and volume. "To think I should be treated in this shoddy way by you, Mere, of all people. It was I who gave you the top job in the best firm in the country. You have lived in luxury in an area renowned for its artistic creativity - the Camelot of the Home Counties. You had a position of trust and were richly rewarded. And then, you despicable toad, you bag of pus, you left me at a time of crisis - and not to any old company but to my deadliest rival right at the peak of a trade war with your head filled with my intended strategy and resources. Not only that, you swine, you took away my wife, my dear, dear, lovely wife."

'He paused for breath. "Well, at least your new employers have recognised you for what you are and have thrown you out, but don't expect any sympathy from me. I hope you rot in this miserable hovel and spend the rest of your life in penury with not a minute in which you don't writhe in anguish remembering your foul behaviour."

'At this point Hector turned and moved towards the prostrate door. Lance's head was on his knees and he was sobbing convulsively. Keith and I were truly distressed to see our old colleague in such a pitiable state and instinctively turned to give him comfort. Hector wouldn't have it. "Come on! Come on!" he shouted and stumbled out of the cottage with Keith and me following meekly after him.

'We climbed into the Long Ranger. "Do you know where there's something called an Earth-life commune?" Hector demanded of the driver.

'"Yes, it's the other side of the lake," said the old boy, "but it's not very nice. I wouldn't go there if I were you."

'"We're going there. Now!" said Hector firmly.

'Neither the lake nor the surrounding countryside were particularly picturesque; on the contrary it was a bleak spot and beloved only by photographers who like to take contrasty black-and-white pictures of ruins or rocky outcrops in a storm. On the far side we could see a ramshackle collection of spavined surface vehicles and gutted planes with a few ragged people moving amongst them. A cauldron was boiling over a fire and some filthy children were playing in the mud. At the sound of our vehicle two packs of dogs approached us from either side of the lake, growling ferociously. Hector, plainly alarmed, called a halt. He cautiously stepped out of the car and came slowly to the edge of the lake.

'"Is Gwendoline Pennington there?" he shouted. "Gwendoline Pennington? Tell her her husband is here."

'There was some conversation amongst the Earth-Livers but no response.

'"Gwendoline!" roared Hector "It's Hector here! I've come to take you back!"

'Was it imagination, or did we see an expensive wimple appear in the window of the grounded plane and perhaps hear a mocking laugh?

'Hector decided to return to the 'Ada Augusta' and resume his siege of the commune the following morning. He reasoned that Gwendoline was not accustomed to roughing it and twenty four hours in close contact with the raggle-taggle gypsies might convince her that her duties lay in Boskey Heath giving support to her husband, encouraging her arty protegés as only she knew how and running the domestic machinery of Dromdeal Tower.'

I can supply the next part of the narrative myself; we will return to Perceval's report later.

Grace was getting restless. She told me she was going to see Lady Iris to seek her advice. I was a little alarmed at this proposal: would not the formidable old lady be hostile to this young woman who, many people supposed, had been the cause of the rift between her son and his wife? I installed myself in my communications cockpit and switched to Lady Iris's drawing room.

Lady Iris rose smartly to her feet and clenched her hands when Miss Halliday's arrival was announced on the homespeaker. I had never seen her so upset, so close to losing control. But Grace's physical presence had the same effect on her as it had had on so many people: the graceful slim figure dressed entirely in white, the round sky-blue eyes, the perfectly formed - almost sex-less - visage, all contributed to the air of tranquillity she radiated. Lady Iris unclenched her fists, seated herself and motioned Grace to do likewise.

"It's good of you to receive me," said Grace, "when you have probably heard some unsavoury rumours about me. I have learned about the disgraceful episode involving Mr Mere and Mrs Pennington and how your son has pursued them into the North country. Let me assure you I have had nothing to do with these events. For the last several weeks I have been with my ballet company in Rome, working very hard."

Lady Iris inclined her head. She said nothing but was clearly softening towards this lily-white damsel.

"The fact is," Grace went on, "I have two urgent tasks to carry out, both of which concern your son. The first is that he asked me to obtain a sample of a unique product from a laboratory in Rome and get it to him as rapidly as possible. I understand that this product, when properly developed and distributed, will have the capability of bringing immense benefits to humanity; so, you can imagine it worries me that it has been in my hands for several days and I still haven't managed to convey it to Mr Pennington."

"And the other task?" Lady Iris asked gently, by now quite in thrall to the young girl.

"My other task is to bring assistance to my ballet troupe who are stranded in Rome and daily in fear of being evicted from their hotels and then thrown into prison. We have run up immense debts which we confidently believed would be met by Mr Teck. His disappearance has put us into a desperate position."

There were several moments' silence whilst Lady Iris reflected gravely.

"As to your first task," she said, with her air of infinite wisdom, "I believe my son's interviewing work has just finished but he hasn't yet returned home. I can understand how reluctant you must be to have this - presumably very valuable - item in your keeping any longer than is necessary. I suggest you travel North and present it to Hector, no matter where he may be... I don't think he will be angry at being interrupted now that he has vanquished the Hadrian Group. You can ask Melvyn how to find him - he seems to know everything that's going on.

"As to your second problem - the settlement of the ballet company's debts and their return from Rome - I greatly fear that we can expect nothing from Josef Teck's estate. I always suspected that a creature of such vulgar extravagance would prove to be a man of straw. Moreover, I very much doubt whether EGCol has sufficient funds in its contingency or reserve accounts to meet the bills. I can spare a little from my private resources but certainly not enough to make up the balance. You will have to leave the problem with me, Miss Halliday. I will have to take action in my position as a major shareholder, and do so quickly. Don't bother any more about your company: concentrate on your first task and take the Ark of the Covenant, or whatever the wretched thing is, to my son." Lady Iris inclined her head to indicate the audience was over. Grace rose from her seat and sinuously departed.

Naturally, I was prepared for Grace's reappearance back at the EGCol office and to give guidance on finding Hector. Her first destination should be, I suggested, the 'Ada Augusta' but if, as I suspected, he wasn't there, I told her how to reach Lance Mere's cottage and, failing that, the Earth-Life commune.

I return to Perceval's report.

'The day day after our emotional scene in Lance's cottage, Hector decided he would go to the lake once again and try to entice his wife to return home with him. Once again we clambered into the old Long Ranger and went to the muddy shores of that desolate lake. Again and again Hector shouted for Gwendoline to talk to him, that all was forgiven, that she could return home with him; each time his call was greeted by the baying of the skinny black dogs and Gwendoline's mocking laugh. Hector was becoming contorted with fury.

'Just as his wrath was at its peak, another ancient car pulled up beside us and, to our astonishment, the slim elegant figure of Grace Halliday emerged and glided towards us carrying a shining silver case. Hector was transfixed with astonishment at this apparition. Grace approached until she was within arm's length and dropped an exquisite curtsy.

'She radiated a brilliant smile. "Chairman," she said, as sweet as a nightingale, "I have pleasure in presenting to you a sample of the extraordinary substance developed by Dr Rex Fischer for you and you alone."

'Hector stood there with his eyes popping and his mouth open, automatically closing his fingers round the handle of the proffered case. Then he raised his head and turned to face the lake again. With a terrifying scream he threw the case as hard as he could into the lake. He seemed to collapse after that. Keith and I took him by the shoulders and led him back to the Long Ranger.

'Grace burst into tears to see the object of her considerable efforts so summarily destroyed. But she pushed aside any attempts to place our consoling arms around her lovely shoulders and eventually followed us in her hired car.

'We rested the remainder of the day in the 'Ada Augusta' with Hector sitting listlessly in front of the artificial fire. Early in the evening Grace, now partly recovered from her rude reception, drew Keith and me aside from our boss.

'"There's something I should tell you," she said. "I called at Mr Mere's cottage on my way to find you this morning. The door had been damaged but had been put back in place. I knocked and knocked but could get no reply. I couldn't see anybody through the window but the light was still on. I thought it was strange, almost sinister."

'After a short discussion with Keith and Hector, who didn't seem to care one way or another, I decided I should go back once again to the cottage. Although it was still bright outside the lamp in the cottage living room was full on. I pushed open the door and went in. There was no-one in the chair where Lance had been weeping yesterday; but his legs were protruding from under the table.

'Lance had had a stroke. His face was twisted mask of brown and purple furrows. His eyes were open but I don't think he recognised me; indeed, I doubt whether he knew there was anyone there at all. We could tell he was alive because his breath was coming in an irregular raucous snore. The driver and I pulled him into the station wagon and took him away.'

CHAPTER EIGHTEEN

Grace Halliday hurried back to Boskey Common and went straight to Lady Iris's roseate cottage; there she told the story of Hector's vain pursuit of his wife, of Lance Mere's stroke and of the watery end of the substance that might have relieved mankind from its evil predilections. A strong bond was developing between the two women: Grace greatly admired the old lady's strength of character and integrity; and Lady Iris's heart was softening towards this graceful guileless girl. Naturally, she was anxious to hear about her son.

"He's been shattered by these events," said Grace, "and he's been in a desperately downcast mood. But Mr Perceval and Mr Kendall are doing their best to revive his spirits so I expect he'll be home in the next day or two."

"I'm sorry he's been so badly affected," said Lady Iris, with little sign of emotion, "but in a way it's good news because it gives us a chance to rescue your ballet company. Not only am I a major shareholder in EGCol, I have the legal right to deploy my son's vote when he is available. I will assume he is unavailable now."

"But," protested the naive Grace, "you can communicate with him quite easily by..."

"Nonsense!" rapped Lady Iris. "I tell you he is incommunicado! I'm going to the EGCol office now."

Within half-an-hour she had installed herself in Hector's office and had videofaxed a request for seventy-two hours' grace to all known debtors of the Princess Ruby Royal Ballet. Keith Kendall's young deputy watched all this activity in amazement. He summoned the courage to speak.

"Excuse me, madam," he asked, " but where are the funds to come from to pay all these debts?"

"It can be done by breaking up EGCol into a number of functional groups," she replied sharply, "and selling off all but the most basic core activities."

"Do you really think you can do that in seventy-two hours?"

"Of course. The company is well-regarded on the international exchange and each unit is independently profitable. What's more it will have been strengthened during the last few days by the acquisition of the Hadrian Group."

"But won't there be a suspicion that something is seriously wrong when the size of the operation becomes known?"

"I shall let it be inferred that a massive amount of cash is needed for a new and extremely ambitious enterprise."

"But isn't that unethic...?"

"Don't be impertinent!"

The young man hurried back to his office and was soon talking to Keith Kendall in Vindolanda. The news aroused Hector from his torpor and he swiftly prepared to leave for home. He made several attempts to videofax his Finance Department to negate his mother's assumption of control but she was prepared for this and promptly erased each message as it arrived in the communications room. Hector could tell by the absence of any 'Message Acknowledgement' signal that his communications were not getting through so he videofaxed his three beautiful aunts urging them to hasten to the EGCol office and stop the old lady's attempt to break up his company.

Hector had still not arrived in Boskey when the three sisters assembled in the EGCol offices, bringing with them Jasper and Mortimer, who each had a few shares in the company. There was pandemonium in Hector's office as all five argued with, then pleaded with, then shouted at Lady Iris to stop this disastrous break-up of the company on which their wealth depended. They hoped that if they could involve the old lady in a dispute for long enough, Hector would arrive and save the situation by re-asserting his authority and reversing her decisions. But she had already drafted documents setting out the missions, the staff resources and the assets of her proposed independent divisions and had contacted a phalanx of brokers. Even as they shouted and screamed, bids were coming in from all over the world for parts of the EGCol empire.

After a quarter-of-an-hour or so of this uproar Mortimer nodded to Jasper to slip out of the room, leaving Lady Iris the increasingly icy target of the sisters' vituperation. I switched to the corridor's transducers. Mortimer, although the younger of the two lads and of weedy physique, had powers of command that his cousin lacked.

"This female caterwauling is achieving nothing," he said. "The old crone won't be deflected by shouts and screams. She will have to be physically restrained."

"D'you have anything in mind?" asked Jasper.

"We could lock her up somewhere. The museum would be a good place, amongst the transparent pavements, the tadpole drying towers and things,"

"But how do we get her there?"

"Simple. We go back into the office and tell her that Hector has arrived and wishes to see her in private and not in front of the three squabbling harridans."

"Steady on. One of those 'harridans', as you call them, is my mother."

"And another is mine. Let's get to work."

They re-entered Hector's office that still resounded to the shrill cries of Morwaine and Elaine, the sardonic contralto of Fay and the husky basso profundo ripostes of Lady Iris. Mortimer edged his way to the old lady.

"Excuse me for interrupting your discussion," he said with no trace of sarcasm, "but I think there is something you should certainly know. Mr Pennington has returned from the North in secrecy and wishes to see you alone in the museum."

The sisters topped squabbling. Perhaps, they thought, Hector intended to divest his mother of her self-assumed powers without embarrassing her in front of his aunts. They remained silent as she muttered a chilly "Excuse me!" and stalked after Mortimer from the room, leaving Jasper to deal with the sisters.

He quickly explained the situation. "This is a bit of a trick," he said. "Hector hasn't come yet, but Mortimer has lured great-aunt down into the museum room so she can't do any further mischief until Hector really does arrive back. He can pick up the reins again and EGCol will survive intact."

"Clever lads!" said Morwaine. "How long can you keep her there?"

"Days and days if need be," said Jasper. "But I don't think that will be necessary. Hector should be here at any time."

As he spoke he felt the slight shudder of a cable-car landing on EGCol's pad. He looked out of the office window and saw Hector, Perceval and Kendall descending from the carriage.

"Excuse me for a moment" he shouted to the sisters and rushed out of the room. He met Mortimer just about to re-enter the office.

"Hector's back!" shouted Jasper.

"Get him down to the museum!" cried Mortimer.

"What for?"

"Don't argue. We must move quickly!"

Mortimer turned and ran back down the stairs to the museum.

Jasper rushed to greet his cousin at the cable pad.

"Hector! Hector! How marvellous to see you. Thank God you're back!"

Hector glared at this strange greeter and searched his memory.

"You're... you're... Jasper, aren't you? What the hell is going on? What's my mother been up to? Where is she now?"

"She's in the museum room with Mortimer."

"What the hell is she doing in the museum room? And who the hell is Mortimer?"

"Your son. They're both down there because... because... some distinguished Malaysian business men have arrived who might bid for one of the EGCol divisions. She's showing them examples of work the company has done in the past."

"There's not going to be any sale of EGCol divisions. I must stop that old battle-cruiser before she does any more harm."

Hector rushed down the stairs, closely followed by Jasper. They found Mortimer at the door of the museum room looking in through the observation window. There was no sign of Lady Iris.

Hector's first words to his son, after an absence of fourteen years, amply demonstrated the depth of his paternal feelings.

"Where's Lady Iris?" he roared.

"She's in the tadpole drying tower."

"What on earth is she doing in there?"

Jasper rapidly intervened. "She's showing how it works to some business men."

"She must be out of her mind. We have plenty of people on the staff who know much more about the details than she does. But I haven't got time to argue. Open the door and let me in."

Mortimer opened the museum room door and followed Hector inside. Jasper apprehensively edged in behind them. He whispered in Mortimer's ear.

"Where is the old lady?"

"In the communications room. When I heard that Hector had arrived I told her that we were mistaken in telling her earlier that he was already here but there was a videogram from him being received right now."

"But why get her out again?"

"I want to get Hector alone in the drying tower."

"Why?"

Mortimer didn't answer but followed his father through the pattern of exhibits to the foot of the tadpole drying tower.

Hector entered through the maintenance door.

"Mother! Mother!" he shouted.

Mortimer clanged the door shut behind him and twisted the handle into the Lock position.

"What are you doing?" cried Jasper.

"Come round to the switchgear," ordered Mortimer. "Now place your hand on this lever and I will place mine of top of yours. Then together we will push the lever steadily upwards."

"But that's the microwave radiation control! You'll kill him! He's your own father!"

"He's never been a father to me. He's treated my mother like dirt. He's an out-and-out swine!"

"But that's no reason to kill him!"

"Don't you realise you idiot, that if Hector dies we two will run the company? The women will own the shares but they will need a manager and that manager must be a Pennington. We'll be able to drop this ethical product nonsense and go flat out for profit - the only reasonable motive there has ever been for a successful business. We can recover all the ground we have lost over these crazy ballet and GRAIL escapades."

"I won't do it!"

Mortimer's skinny frame was convulsed by the power of his hatred. His hand gripped Jasper's and began to move the lever. Jasper struggled but he couldn't slow Mortimer's inexorable drive. The lever was now quite vertical; the microwave heater was at full power. Shouts and thumps could be heard from within the tower; after a few minutes they became intermittent, then stopped. Mortimer released his grip on Jasper's hand and the level fell back to the OFF position.

I had watched this scene in incredulous horror, quite unable to do anything to save the man who, despite his faults, I had served with unswerving loyalty since his childhood. The two young murderers stood by the tower for a few minutes, Mortimer white-faced, Jasper weeping uncontrollably. When the heater had cooled down, Mortimer opened the tower door and watched impassively as a figure in smoking clothes, headed by a great cracked brown blister, slumped out on to the floor.

Ten minutes later Mortimer re-appeared in Hector's office where the three sisters were waiting impatiently for Hector or his mother. He sidled across the room and stood beside Elaine.

"Mother," he said calmly, "I fear there's been a dreadful accident."

Fay scrabbled through Hector's office cupboard until she found the SCABBARD machine and rushed down to the museum room. With her face averted from the revolting sight, she placed the pads where her nephew's temples used to be. She typed in 'Radiation Burns' and stood back. Nothing happened. I arrived at the museum room just as the reeking corpse was being carried away and managed to rescue the machine from under the feet of the rapidly gathering crowd. I opened the case and looked at the slot where the programme module should be; there was nothing there.

CHAPTER NINETEEN

I had always admired Lady Iris but now my esteem grew beyond all measure. Although stricken with grief by the frightful death of her only son and having taken full responsibility for the funeral arrangements, she still maintained her icy composure and worked without pause to release the ballet company from its burden of debt. Within three days she had sold the transparent pavement, the helium balloon and the tadpole protein divisions and had sent bankers' drafts to the hotels, theatrical equipment suppliers, costumiers, transport companies and everyone else who had provided goods and services so lavishly to the company. By the fourth day, and in time for Hector's funeral, a bedraggled stream of dancers, musicians and dressers were arriving back in Boskey Common from their adventures in Rome. Grace met as many as she could to thank them personally for their efforts and their endurance of a rapidly-deteriorating situation and to offer them places in her new company; but most of them politely declined - their one experience of a Pennington/Halliday artistic venture had been quite enough.

Only I knew in detail how Hector had died and the parts that Mortimer and Jasper had played in his death but I believe Lady Iris suspected that evil forces had been at work. The two boys, of course, maintained it had all been a fearful accident - that Hector had rushed into the tower looking for his mother and that they only discovered his location when they heard his dying screams from inside. He had probably inadvertently brushed against the microwave switchgear in his impetuosity. They had released him - at no small risk to themselves - but it was then too late. They were, naturally, desolated by the tragedy.

Lady Iris listened to this account with scarcely a twitch to her tragic mask. By the logic she herself had applied when she appointed Hector to the chairmanship of the company, the new leader had to be a male Pennington, either Jasper or Mortimer(I had no doubt in my mind who it would ultimately be, no matter who took up the position in the first instance). But she managed to defer any immediate appointment by saying it would be improper for anyone to take Hector's position, certainly before his funeral and preferably not until after a period of mourning. The contenders accepted this decision with ill grace; meanwhile each urged his mother to present his splendid attributes to Lady Iris and other major shareholders in the most enhancing way.

The day of Hector's funeral was declared an official day of mourning and all but the most essential work in Boskey Common was closed down. Hector's body was laid out in long white and golden robes on a catafalque positioned at the east end of Charlie's Fields so that the good people of Boskey could file past and pay their last respects. The frightful nature of his demise was concealed by tucking his twisted and blistered hands into the long sleeves of his robe and by covering the horror that had once been his face by a Greek mask of tragedy. Lady Pennington, dressed in purple, with a long black veil draped over her wimple and features, sat impassively on the throne at one end of the field.

When she had decided that these humble acts of homage had gone on long enough, she signed to the stewards to clear the ground and move everyone back beyond the side ropes. Solemn music dirged through the loudspeakers. From some distant cabin, where it had remained in waiting for many years, the purple and black funeral cable-car of the Penningtons swung slowly into view and touched down at the Charlie's Fields terminal. The four remaining directors of EGCol, together with Jasper and Mortimer, lifted Hector's body on its stretcher and slowly, reverently, slid it into the funeral car. Then they turned and took their places besides Lady Iris's throne. The music ceased and a thrilling trumpet call filled the arena. From behind the throne there emerged the three sisters, Morwaine entirely in white, Elaine in purple and Fay in black. The crowd exclaimed in wonder: never had such shattering beauty been seen since The Most Famous Film Star in the World had carried off Laurence in her de Havilland Rapide all those years ago. All eyes turned back to the throne: would

Gwendoline appear to make up a quartet of lovelies? She did not.

The funeral car shuddered and started to move slowly from the terminal. The three sisters strode slowly behind in line abreast, legs and arms moving in perfect unison, heads bowed at the same graceful angle. Then, as the car gathered speed, they boarded it in one swift motion and, with the silent crowds below gazing up in awe, some on their knees, some with hands clasped as if to a long-for gotten deity, they swooped aloft in a bowed mourning arc round the corpse of EGCol's most celebrated citizen.

CHAPTER TWENTY

Looking back over these chronicles, I grieve to perceive how EGCol, which had started out under young Hector with such noble principles and high ambitions, later became the arena for conflict, treachery and murder. But, then, that's life.

Perhaps the most tragic figure to survive was Lady Iris Pennington. She had become increasingly certain that her only son, the living force behind EGCol, had been killed by her two nephews, but she realised she couldn't mete out just punishment without creating a fearful public scandal. The most she could do was to delay their being appointed to senior positions in the management of EGCol by insisting on an indefinitely long period of family mourning. She retired to her beautiful cottage and was never seen outside its walls again. I was her only visitor. Even her three beautiful step-sisters never called upon her: they were never invited. I became so embarrassed at having a surveillance outlet in her living room focussed on her as she sat there motionless, hour after hour, that I disconnected the line and never monitored her in her home again.

Almost as pitiful was Lance Mere who was confined to a wheelchair and installed in a nursing home in Wallsend. One of my colleagues in EGCol's northern office visited him and reported that Lance, once one of the most vigorous and positive-minded of men, was now little more than a vegetable in distorted human form. At least, that was one's first impression: but after spending a little time with him, listening to his grunts and slurred words, watching his slobbering mouth and the jerky movements of his eyes, one became aware that there was still an intelligence operating inside that contorted frame. All the wheelchairs in the nursing home were equipped with their own TV receivers and headphones so that the patients had access to every cable and broadcast channel. Lance would wrestle painfully against the chaotic forces controlling his nervous system in order to find the programme of his choice, only for a passing nurse to say "Oh, you don't want that old rubbish, do you?" and switch to the 24-hour sports channel. Lance hated sport. His concept of hell, which he suffered in reality every day, was a desperate search for something that was intellectually or artistically stimulating, and then have it over-ridden by the kindly staff and replaced by the brain-deadening vacuities of basket-ball, golf, horse-riding and all the other muscular grotesqueries of man and beast. He would struggle for hours against the disobedient movements of his own arms and hands to find some music or mathematics, then be frustrated by some well-intentioned nurse switching back to sport again. "Silly old you!" they would say playfully, as though to a small boy, "Why do you have to keep messing around with your great clumsy fingers when I have already set it up for the football?"

The components of the mysterious substance that Dr Fischer had created and that had been flung by a wrathful Hector into the lake were never known outside the Vatican laboratory, but they certainly had a collective potency; within three days the lake had changed from its normal mud colour into a shimmering turquoise bluey-green. The Earth-Lifers were cautious at first but, after a few days of life without water, they resumed using it for their daily cooking pots and monthly baths. Within a week they had all changed in character: gone were the days of quarrels, harsh words and fisticuffs: now all was sweetness and light, mutual help and sunny smiles. Even the dogs didn't bark or snarl, but greeted strangers by wagging their tails and rolling on their backs for their tummies to be tickled. Everyone was suffused with Goodness.

Gwendoline, perhaps because she bathed more frequently than her fellows, was more affected than anyone else in the commune. She founded an order of pan-religious nuns and clothed herself in a shapeless jute sack which completely concealed her lovely presence. Her pure melodious voice, once the instrument for celebrating erotic joys, was now confined to carolling songs of praise and psalms of the most sickening religiosity. The local cable TV network, realising it had a star within its own franchise area, gave her a nightly slot in their UFG

(Universal Force for Good) channel. The care-assistants at Lance's nursing home soon learnt that this warbling angel had once been his sweetheart and made sure that his receiver was tuned to her concert every evening. "There now, look how the poor dear is enjoying it," they chortled as he writhed and gibbered in his chair. "He's re-united in song with his loved one!" And they smiled in their sincerely caring fashion as he fried in a hell even more excoriating than sport.

With the assistance of some of her original Borealis Dance troupe and a few of the Princess Ruby ballet who hadn't been too scarred by their experiences in Rome, Miss Halliday formed a new company called Grace and Favourites. Her ambition was modest: it was to tour the smaller towns of England which had never seen a live performance in the last thirty years and where the audiences could, as she put it "... open the windows of their souls to the Magic of the Dance." In spite of her triumphs in Rome, the Princess Ruby episode had soured her appreciation of contemporary works and she expunged everything of the twenty-first century from her repertoire. Indeed, only two from the twentieth century were admitted: Fokine's 'Les Sylphides' and Ashton's 'Symphonic Variations' - a choice indicative of her modesty since neither gave the prima ballerina an outstanding solo role.

There must be many thousands of village halls and derelict bingo-houses scattered over England, so I suppose she can continue bringing cut-price culture to the masses well into her middle age: then, perhaps, she will settle down with an insurance broker or some such respectable person.

Company directors Kendall, Perceval and Wain strove hard to make a viable business from what one might call EGCol's pre-Hector range of goods and services; and, indeed, there were indications that the company - although but a glimmer of its former glory - would soon be profitable again. Mortimer made no secret of his impatience to take control and of his frustration at the hurdles Lady Iris was putting in his way. Bovine Jasper was but an echo of his cousin's ambitions.

I was sitting in my little surveillance room one day, idly flicking through the channels - although, to be honest, there wasn't much of interest to survey - when I received a call on my personal videophone. To my astonishment it was Lady Iris "I want you to come to my cottage straight away," she said. I went.

She was sitting as stiff as a post in her armchair, her hands folded in her lap, her face lined with sorrow but her eyes shining like an eagle's. Her dress was black with white lace round her throat and cuffs: she was a Rembrandt come to life. She directed me to a seat directly in front of her and said: "You always seem to know what's going on, so you will be aware that that young villain, my grandson Mortimer, is desperately trying to take control of EGCol. He proposes to share the posts of Chairman and Managing Director with his idiot cousin, Jasper, but I don't need to tell you that that situation wouldn't last very long. If I were Jasper I would reserve tickets to an obscure part of the globe as soon as I could.

"Once Mortimer has EGCol in his grasp, his greed will know no limits. He will discard our tradition of always dealing in ethical products and services, he will cut the staff to a minimum and drive up profits to a maximum; and he will expand exports to poor countries and extort payment by demanding the import of raw materials at well below their market price. He will besmirch the good name of EGCol, of which my son and I were so proud, and it will never recover."

"All this is true," I murmured.

"I am not going to allow it to happen!" cried Lady Iris, with a sudden burst of fury. "It will not happen and you are to be my agent to prevent it from happening. You must destroy EGCol whilst it is still universally regarded with respect."

"Destroy EGCol!" I shouted. "I can't do that! It has been my life's work! What of all the employees? What will happen to them?"

"I am going to write or speak to every one of them to say I will present them with a handsome redundancy payment provided they undertake to start up their own businesses (either individually or in partnership with their colleagues) which adhere to EGCol's noble principles. Besides giving them a new start in life, this will give me an incentive to continue living. You will be my contact with the outside world: you will examine their business plans, check them for financial viability and advise me whether or not to provide their initial funding.

"So, you see, you needn't worry that your life's work will be destroyed. It will re-appear in a thousand different seedlings."

"I see," I said doubtfully, "but how can I - very much on the margin, these days - destroy EGCol?"

"Think back," she said, "to those exciting three days when Hector, little more than a boy, first took control."

I thought back and understood. I rose and kissed her hand, "It shall be done," I said.

Of course! The whole of EGCol's communications, data storage and manipulation processes still depended on the opto-electronic module which Hector had himself inserted into the data control centre all those years ago. Hector - perhaps realising the power that it gave him - had forbidden that it should ever be replaced or duplicated. Without it, EGCol's nervous system would go berserk. But how could I remove it without being seen or otherwise drawing suspicion upon myself? I sought the participation of Lady Iris.

On the last day of the month a fax in her ladyship's imperious hand was received in the communications centre requiring all EGCol staff to assemble in the conference room at 15.00 GMT: she was to make an important announcement about the future of the company. As you might imagine, this caused immense excitement and the conference centre was crammed with chattering EGCol employees well before the appointed time. Jasper and Mortimer were sitting in the front row, Jasper beaming all over his great round face, Mortimer betraying his anticipation of his long-awaited appointment by a lop-sided smirk and a gleam in his colourless eyes. I mingled with the staff at the back of the hall, chatting to whoever could be bothered to talk to me.

At 15.00 precisely the great 2500-line screen at the end of the room flashed up a caption: "A message from Lady Iris Pennington", to be immediately followed by her austere countenance. As soon as she started to speak in her firm bass voice, I quietly extricated myself from the cluster of people I had been with and slipped out the rear door. No-one saw me go: all attention was on the screen. I was greatly disappointed at missing seeing the expressions on the faces of the two pretenders to the EGCol throne as it gradually dawned on them that this was not an announcement of their accession; but I was working on cue and had no time to spare. I entered the deserted computer room as Lady Iris was nearing the end of her peroration and activated two monitors: one showed the same picture of her delivering her speech as was being seen in the conference centre and the other of of her open-mouthed audience. It was one of the most stirring moments of my life to see the astonishment of the employees as they learned they were to be funded to start up their own businesses; and the fury of Mortimer and the blank incomprehension of Jasper as they realised the old lady had thwarted them once again was undiluted joy. I was relishing the spectacle so much I almost missed my cue : for Lady Iris was saying:

"... as I say these final words, EGCol will cease to exist. Goodbye!"

I strode to the control cabinet, opened it with my master key and pulled out the opto-electronic module that Hector had inserted with his own hands when still but a callow lad. Instantly the incoming faxes and data print-outs turned to garbage, the visual displays became meaningless swirling patterns and the messages to and fro EGCol's national and international subsidiaries were convulsed into a hopeless jumble. The company's nervous system had been destroyed: EGCol would never operate again.

I slipped the module into the pocket of my cloak and joined the other staff as they poured out of the conference centre.

I spent a highly emotional evening back in the converted chapel I call my home. I cried until there were runnels down my face to think that I, I of all people, had just destroyed an entity that was more than just a commercial company: it was almost a family of like-minded spirits, a sponsor of the arts, the champion of the down-trodden, almost

- perhaps a touch fancifully - tending towards the ideal city-state. Then I rejoiced to think it was I who had committed euthanasia on a body that had started so nobly but had fallen into sour decay; and that it was I who had thwarted the rascally descendants of a celebrated family.

So I laughed and cried alternately for several hours until I did the only sensible thing one can do under such circumstances: got drunk.

CHAPTER TWENTY ONE

(Found in the undergrowth on Edgemore Heath)

I'm recording this on my pocket cassette notebook; I'll transcribe it on to something more substantial later and tidy up the grammar a bit.

I awoke this morning with a vile headache and a mouth like the Kalahari desert, complete with Hottentots. Thought I'd better look at myself to ascertain whether I was fit to be seen in public. Took me ages to find a mirror - it was underneath a pile of old cloaks and under garments in the undercroft. They were covered with a sort of orange fungus and smelled of long-dead mice. There's nothing for it: they'll have to be burned. There was a mould covering the mirror and I had to rub the glass with my cloak-sleeve for several minutes before it started to work properly and look back at me.

I had the shock of my life. I'm old!

Of course I know I'm old in terms of the number of decades, perhaps even centuries, I've lived through, but I've always managed to convince myself that I carried my years well and that I was generally regarded as a sprightly elderly chap. But the creature staring back at me was straggly-bearded, wrinkled, nearly bald, bleary-eyed, deeply lined, blotchy, scaly and repulsively ugly. I tried to re-assure myself that the bleary eyes were the consequences of last night's binge, but even if they recovered and became as clear as a mountain pool - an unlikely scenario - the rest of the countenance would still be horrid. I should have known: there's no reason why the years shouldn't have left their stain on me just as they do on the rest of humanity. In fact, now that I have caught a glimpse of the real me, I have to acknowledge that I might be expected to be worse off than most... I've lived an unhealthy life... always indoors... little natural lighting... snatching a meal of spicey-flavoured pabulum at any time of day or night... experimenting with every stimulus that has been invented...

And here was the result: a bent, bowed old bugger, a still from an ancient film about the living dead. I was surprised the people in EGCol had tolerated me for so long - I had even attending Board meetings and no-one had remarked upon my repulsive appearance! And Lady Iris, that impeccable model of elegance, had permitted me to sit before her in her lovely cottage when she would have been justified in taking me up in tongs and depositing me in the garbage disposal machine.

I was sitting in my little living room with my head in my hands, groaning heavily, when a call came through on my videophone. Another shock!... it was Fay!... more beautiful, more entrancing, more entrail-liquefying than ever! I pulled my cloak over my head and emitted stifled sobbing noises.

"Melvyn! Whatever is the matter?" said Fay, in her brown velvet voice. Why can't I look at you?"

"I'm not fit to be seen," I sniffled.

"Not fit?... Ridiculous! You're an old sweetie! You're my favourite business adviser!"

"Oh, god, Fay!" I sobbed. "Please don't taunt me! Please go away!"

"I shall certainly not go away! Quite the reverse. I called to tell you that I'm coming to pay you a visit. I'll be with you in a quarter of an hour. Do pull yourself together."

I rushed to the bathroom and subjected myself to a shower of liquid lanolin, raked my fingers through my beard and my vestiges of hair and put on a new - or new-ish cloak. I dared not look in the mirror again; I just hoped I was a tiny bit more presentable than I had been earlier in the morning.

Fay's voice came through the Home Announcer. I was trembling with embarrassment. I could scarcely stand up when she entered the room. I had never been so close to her as this before and my senses were overloaded by the perfection of her features, the sheen of her blacker-than-black hair, her huge gleaming eyes, the pallor of her skin and the power of her animal sexuality which she radiated as stove radiates heat.

"How lovely to see you in the flesh," she murmured. "D'you know, I believe this is the first opportunity we've had of chatting together.

What a lot of time we've wasted!"

"Fay," I stuttered, emboldened by sheer nervousness, "Fay, I've admired you from afar since the first time I saw you. I think it was at Sir Arthur's funeral."

"What a shaft of happy memories you must have, Melvyn," said Fay, with only a trace of sarcasm, "but why didn't you tell me then?"

"Oh, really, Fay!" I spluttered. "How could I? You, one of the most celebrated members of a distinguished family and me, but an ugly old functionary! Even uglier now!"

"Don't go on about ugliness, you dear old thing. Don't you know that only the coarsest type of woman is impressed by good looks? The more discerning amongst us value intelligence, imagination, authority, experience... and you had... no! I should say 'have'... all those qualities in abundance."

"Oh, really, Fay!" I said again.

"And haven't you heard of the aphrodisiac of power?" Fay was sidling closer; I was becoming so overheated by the nearness of her radiation I expected my cloak to start smouldering.

"Power?" I gurgled. "What power?"

"The power of life or death over a mighty company," she said, still in her seductive contralto voice. "The power to start up EGCol again. The power to re-insert the module and get the computer room ticking away... and see all your old friends and colleagues back at work in one of the world's most successful enterprises."

"But, Fay!" I spluttered. "What makes you think that I..."

She laughed in my face. "Who else would know how to do it, you clever old bird? You fooled everyone but me, although I don't suppose it was your original idea. I bet that old witch, Iris, was behind it. But you've got the key, the module... and don't forget I have a right to it... it was my design in the first place."

"If it was your design, why don't you make another one?"

"Idiot! That was twenty years ago. You know very well that skill like that dies after a few years if it hasn't been regularly exercised. It can't be resurrected. Come on,. hand it over!"

I recoiled, shaking my head. In a flash she was on me, sinking her hands in my cloak pockets. Fortunately it was a newly-donned cloak so she found nothing.

I collapsed on a chair, overcome by the shock of her assault; (but there was a part of me that found that wrestling with Fay wasn't altogether unpleasant).

She released me and stepped back, shaking her head as though ashamed of her behaviour.

"What am I thinking of?" she said. "This is no way to behave. I must have become obsessed by that stupid module. Let's put the whole tiresome business behind us and start again from the beginning. You will forgive me, won't you?"

"Willingly!" I choked, melting once again in her aura.

"Let me make amends," she suggested. "Come and spend the evening with me. I can conjure up some superb exotic dishes and I have a cellar full of rare fine wines that no-one else in this ghastly dreary town has heard of, let alone savoured. And I can waft some ancient romantic music over you - played on the original instruments - that will have you swooning with ecstasy You will come, won't you? Do say 'yes'".

I nearly swooned there and then. An evening with Fay! How could I refuse?

"Oh, yes, yes!" I cried. "Thank you, Fay, delighted."

"I'll call for you at eight," she said, and swept out of my home.

Some fragments of sanity came back to me during the day. Fay was widely suspected of being a witch, a skilled dispenser of noxious potions, a hypnotist and much besides. Of course, she hadn't given up her search for the module as readily as she seemed. Her succulent dishes and fine wines would undoubtedly be riddled with drugs which would strike me senseless whilst she returned to my dwelling and searched for the module from cellar to eaves. But it was no good my refusing to go with her now that I had already accepted her invitation.

In any case, to turn down the chance of a tete-a-tete with the object of my carnal desires was unthinkable... I decided to hide the module and honour my assignation.

It took me three hours to think of a suitable hiding place. It was no use trying conventional ideas such as dangling it in a cistern, thrusting it in pot of peanut butter, or in a hollowed-out book or the heel of a shoe or a pot in the garden... Fay was bound to think of all of those. Eventually I had the bright idea of taking it with me; so I tucked it in the bobble of my long woolly cap.

It's just past eight-o-clock and I'm fluttering with excitement. Fay was only a few minutes late and is leading me by the hand to the cable-car stop at the end of my lane. She has brought her own car: the outside gleams with purple enamel and bears her family crest; the interior is covered - walls, floor, ceiling - with scarlet plush. Our journey lasted about fifteen minutes and we have pulled into her car-port. I gasp at its novelty - it's on top of a low hill surrounded by trees. More overhead cables indicate there must be other dwellings nearby but they are lost in the woods. Fay is leading me by the hand down steps cut into the hillside. I'm astonished by how rural everything is... I expected something much more sophisticated. We turn and now we are at the entrance to a cave and beside the cave is a pool. I stop briefly and gaze into the pool. For the second time today I see that sad raddled face... I'm old!... I'm old!

I'm trembling with apprehension. Fay gives my sleeve a jerk and tugs me towards the cave.

"What's the matter?" she asks, smiling her tigerish smile, "Didn't you know I lived in a cave?"

She tugs my sleeve again. I feel sick with horror. I follow her in, unable to resist.

I know this is the end.

FAMILY TREE.

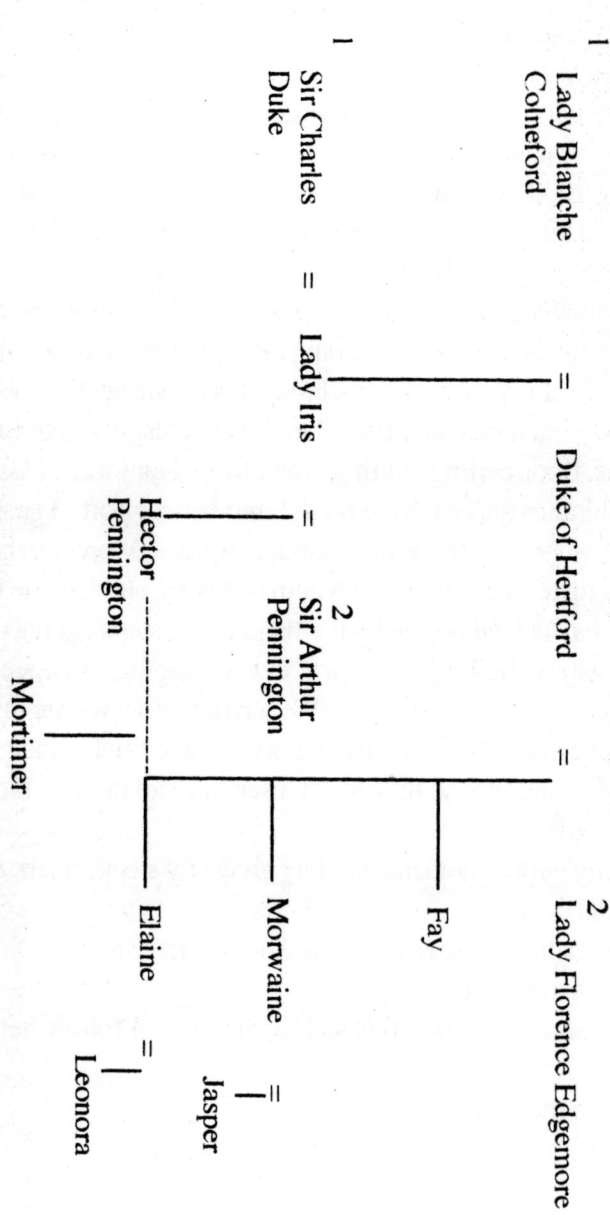

170